*Staying Afloat*

Sue Wilsea was born in Portsmouth in 1952, and now lives in East Yorkshire. During the last thirty years she has taught English in schools, colleges, libraries, community centres, prisons, and at present, on the part-time Creative Writing degree at the University of Hull.

Her writing has been widely published, broadcast and performed, and her accolades include being one of nine writers labelled 'New and Gifted' by the Jerwood/Arvon Foundation in 2010. She has won a BBC radio competition for multi-episode short stories, and been shortlisted for the Bridport Prize. Her first collection of short stories, *Blood Sisters*, was published by Stone Creek Press in 1993.

# Staying Afloat

## SUE WILSEA

*VALLEY*

First published 2012 by Valley Press
Woodend, The Crescent, Scarborough, YO11 2PW
www.valleypressuk.com

ISBN: 978 1 908853 12 7
Cat. no. VP0030

9 8 7 6 5 4 3 2

A CIP record for this book is
available from the British Library

Printed and bound in Great Britain by
Imprint Digital, Upton Pyne, Exeter

www.valleypressuk.com/authors/suewilsea

*for Zannie, Jamie, Kate and Ollie*

# Acknowledgements

A number of these stories originally formed part of the collection *Blood Sisters*. 'Two Ophelias and Me' was published in *QWF*, 'Listening' in *Iron* magazine and 'Seeing the Light' in Route's anthology *The Unexpected Pond*. A multi-episode version of 'Paper Flowers' won a BBC radio competition, and was read on air by Dame Judi Dench.

# Contents

# Shapes. Colours.

Every morning started with sharing circle time. As soon as all Class 6's coats were hung up on the pegs outside – the puffa jackets, fleeces, shiny raincoats, the oversized hand-me-downs – they sat cross-legged on the scratchy bit of carpet in front of Miss Anderson's desk and put a finger over their mouths to seal them shut. When everyone was there and Miss Anderson had called the register, she pointed at the thermometer chart and asked each of them how they felt. The thermometer was filled with blocks of colour, with bright yellow at the top and dark blue-black at the bottom. Yellow had lots of nice words like 'happy' and 'excited' whereas blue-black had words like 'miserable' and 'sad'. Each child's name was printed onto a piece of card which had Velcro on the back so it could be stuck onto the right colour. Most days there were lots of names on yellow, red and orange because if you said you felt like a dark word then Miss Anderson and the rest of the class would ask you what was the matter and how could they help.

Stephen knew for a fact that some of the girls made things up so they could be the centre of attention. But he made sure he was always smiling at circle time and always amongst the sunshine colours. He loved Miss Anderson dearly and couldn't bear the thought of leaving her when he went to Big School next September; but it was because he loved her that he didn't want to burden her with his Worry. Miss Anderson was Irish and had a lovely, soothing voice. When they said their prayers at going home time he would bend his head like the others but squint one eye open to watch her soft lips shape the words.

His Worry had started as just a tiny spider of anxiety, scuttling around in his head at night when he couldn't sleep. But recently it had been growing, like his mother's tumour had done, and it bothered him most of his waking hours. Stephen's Worry was that his father, who had always been eccentric, was now completely mad. As a very young child he had honestly believed that all fathers spent their days combing the riverbank for fossils, bringing any finds home to add to the stacks of newspapers, magazines, books, records, shoeboxes full of old index card systems and junk shop purchases with which their small house was stuffed. But it didn't take long for him to gauge from his visits to friends' houses that this was not normal. Other people's fathers went out to work in the week and at weekends took their sons out to do things like play football in the park. Going out to work meant there was money, which paid for kitchens with polished worktops and bedrooms with boxes full of toys and things painted on the wall: his friend Tommy had a desert island with palm trees, and his bed was shaped like a pirate ship.

Apparently when Stephen was a baby his father had worked: in the library, not in the part where they lend you books but in the part where people go to find things out. When Stephen asked why he stopped working there his father's eyes had gone all watery and he said that, if Stephen didn't mind, he'd prefer not to talk about it. Perhaps he'd just got too old, for he was much older than other kids' fathers. Tommy's Dad, for example, looked more like an older brother than a Dad. That was another thing; Stephen's father wasn't a Dad. Dads wore suits in the week and jogging bottoms and trainers at the weekend. They liked sport and drank pints of beer at the pub. With his white hair and beard, Stephen's father looked like Santa Claus, except he wasn't fat and jolly like Santa Claus – he was thin and sad looking.

But Mum was definitely a Mum, so normal that it had

always balanced things out, and Stephen, who loved Maths, thought of the three of them as an isosceles triangle with him and Mum being the two equal angles at the bottom. Mum worked at the local Co-op and laughed and joked with other kids' Mums. She used to play down her husband's strange ways, saying that it would be a very dull world if everyone was the same and that all geniuses had been thought odd in their time. Stephen didn't think his father was a genius.

'Stephen?'

He flinched. 'What?'

There were stifled giggles from some of the girls. 'I beg your pardon, not what, Stephen.' Although Miss Anderson was telling him off, her voice was gentle. 'I asked what colour you were feeling like today?'

'Light orange,' Stephen said. He had learned that the best way to avoid suspicion was to not always go for the top colours. Also to make eye contact, which he did now.

Miss Anderson gave him one of her probing looks, but moved on to Sophie who said that she was grey so she had an excuse to talk about her gerbil's eye infection. But he hadn't escaped that easily. When playtime bell went, Miss Anderson asked him to stay behind; and when the rest of the class had trooped out, many throwing curious glances their way, she sat down beside him at one of the small tables and asked him how he and his father were coping. Stephen was thrown into panic both by the question itself and by the fact that he could smell his teacher's warmth and perfume so close to him that it made his chest feel tight and his breaths come quickly. Out of the corner of his eye he could see the swell of her small breasts under her jumper and he longed to lay his head on them.

'I just wondered because he didn't come to Parents Evening last week, and I do appreciate how difficult life must be for the two of you right now.'

'He's fine, miss.'

'Are you sure now Stephen?'

'Yes, miss.'

'You know I'm always here if you want to talk, don't you Stephen?'

'Yes, miss. Can I go out to play now?'

She sighed and stood up. He sensed that he'd disappointed her somehow. 'Yes, off you go. But don't forget that you and your father are in my prayers.'

Stephen found a corner of the playground where he could be alone and crouched down, hugging his knees. He needed to think about the previous evening, when he and his father had gone down to the foreshore, as they did most evenings. The Humber was not like the rivers you get in storybooks which are a lovely sapphire blue and wind like snakes through lush, green countryside. Their river was a sludgy brown, long and broad, rolling like the back of a huge animal towards the North Sea. As they made their way down to the shoreline his father continually muttered to himself, and occasionally wrung his hands together as if some great tragedy had just happened. Which of course it had. His Mum's illness had been quick and terrible: only four months from diagnosis to her death. He had watched his father crumble, just like the ragged cliffs above them which month by month were being eroded by the river and the wind. Then last night, after scurrying here and there in a way that reminded Stephen of their neighbour's highly-strung dog, his father had spotted something on the sand and had gone down on all fours to examine it. Luckily it was late and no one else seemed to be about; but Stephen, standing a short distance away, kept looking over his shoulder in case anyone he knew suddenly appeared. A strong breeze, bringing a chill to the summer evening, had picked up and he shivered. Then his father jumped to his feet, and Stephen thought he shouted *Eureka*, but he might have imagined it because last week Miss Anderson had been teaching them about Archimedes and all that stuff was still inside his head. Brandishing a small rock, his father stumbled over the sand and as he drew closer Stephen could see how wild his eyes were and how his cheeks were flushed as if he had a fever. He remembered how Mum used to press a damp flannel to his forehead when he had a fever and how, in a strange sort of way, that made it nice to be poorly.

'I've found it! I've found it at last!' his father gabbled, thrusting his face in front of Stephen's, but Stephen knew that his father wasn't really seeing him so he didn't even have to pretend to listen to his father explaining that he had found a Bronze Age fossil that would prove beyond doubt that there were some ancient remains worth excavating on the foreshore.

'Come on Pops.'

Taking his father's arm, Stephen led him back up the steps to the lane which ran parallel to the river and on to which their house backed. Shoving the rickety gate open, he was suddenly aware of how quickly everything had deteriorated. At the same time the previous year, when Mum was alive and well, the little back yard had been punctuated with splashes of colour like daubs of paint on canvas; three terracotta pots, one smaller than the other two and planted with pale pink and yellow roses, stood together on the paved area. *Just like our family* Mum used to joke. On the side of the shed hung two cone-shaped baskets spilling over with lots of flowers whose names Stephen didn't know, while a box under the kitchen window was packed tightly with pansies, her favourite flowers, their velvety purple and pink petals fluttering in the draught from the open kitchen window. Mum would often be at the window washing up when he returned from school, the radio blasting out some awful old pop tunes, and she would give him a wave as he opened the back gate. Washing always seemed to be flapping on the line, and on the days Mum was at work Stephen would bury his face in clean sheets and towels, loving their fresh, tangy smell.

But now, looking round, he saw that there was only dry grey stuff in the pots and baskets, while the empty washing line sagged as if it too couldn't bear the loneliness. The window of the shed had a large crack zig-zagging across it, and there was dog dirt all over the path.

Stephen unlocked the back door and ushered in his father, who was still tenderly cradling the rock in his hands, stroking it and talking at high speed about other famous discoveries, something about The British Museum and receiving the OBE from the Queen. But anyone could see that it was just a stupid, ordinary bit of rock he was holding, and so great was Stephen's urge to hit his father that he had to screw his eyes up tightly to blank out a vision of the helpless figure on the ground. It was at that moment that he realised the Worry was too big for him to cope with and that he would have to hand it over to someone else.

The next morning he told the circle he was feeling grey and said that he didn't want to share it with the rest of the class but would explain to Miss Anderson afterwards. She held his hand while he did so and then said that he had been a very brave, kind boy and must now place his trust in the Lord.

The hospital where they took his father was a dirty cream colour. The walls were dirty cream and so were the sheets on his bed. His father shared a room with three other men: one dribbled and talked nonsense, one just stared into space and said nothing while the third sounded and acted completely normal. That was until one visiting time when Stephen witnessed the man attacking his wife with a vase of flowers and had to press the alarm bell, which resulted in two nurses rushing in and hauling the man out. The man's wife had cried and there was broken glass and water and red carnations, like clots of blood, all over the floor. His father didn't appear to notice all the drama. He was much calmer now, spending most of his time staring out of the window by his bed, which looked onto the car park and a row of wheelie bins. The only time he became agitated was when anyone touched his precious rock, which stood on his bedside locker, an ugly misshapen lump of brown nothingness.

Stephen himself was placed with foster parents, who were Miss Anderson's aunt and uncle and not unkind. They prayed a lot and he went to Mass with them twice on Sundays and once mid-week. On Saturdays they took him to the hospital to visit his father who was apparently 'making good progress', but whenever Stephen asked about going home everyone changed the subject. On his bed in his new home, Stephen had a patchwork quilt made up of squares of material in all different patterns and colours. His foster parents had looked after a lot of children over the years and a new square had been added with each child. Soon after he'd arrived, he'd been asked to choose his bit of material from a large box of remnants, but he lied and said he was colour blind.

The following Spring Miss Anderson got married, and she looked so beautiful in her snow-white dress, carrying a bouquet of yellow roses, that it gave Stephen an ache in his heart. She gave him a kiss on his head which, although embarrassing, was the first kiss he'd had in a long time so was nice. He wasn't asked to be in any of the many photographs that were taken afterwards on the lawn of the smart hotel. Miss Anderson had six little bridesmaids, and Stephen watched as the photographer arranged them sitting in a circle around the billowing folds of her dress.

Come September, when he went to Big School, they didn't have circle time anymore and Stephen was glad, knowing that he didn't ever want to be part of a circle again. Instead they had assemblies where they sat in rows, youngest at the front and sixth-formers at the back, and were told things by teachers with shouty voices. Slowly but surely Stephen disappeared inside his head, allowing it to fill with numbers and letting his childhood memories fade until they became just bleached bones of driftwood on a distant shore.

# Other Side of the Island

'Puffing Billy' brought us home every day from our school on the mainland. It steamed over Langton Bridge where, at low tide, small rowing boats lay beached like warts on ridged and folded skins of mud.

A swarm of greenbottles, boatered and capped, we heaved down the sooty windows to lean out and holler as the train rounded the last bend before the station – real St. Trinian's stuff. Then, with a great juddering and squealing, brakes were applied, the train slowed and a platform rose up to devour the wild-flowered embankment on our right hand side. A jolt, one final exhausted hiss, and with what always seemed to be miraculous accuracy the engine came to a standstill just inches away from the buffers. Whacking back the doors, we erupted from our dusty second-class carriages eager to set foot on our island again.

'Now then, you lot. No running along the platform.'

Mr Lowe, the stationmaster. We knew all the drivers and stokers by name.

'Miss Jennifer, your mother says to meet her at the hairdressers if you please.'

They all lived on the island, most of them on a council estate kept immaculate with regular coats of fresh white paint.

'Tickets please!'

A different breed to those British Rail employees who worked at Lime Street. At least our friends could get their skins clean at the end of the day, I once heard my father say.

'It's four thirty-two, young man, so your taxi won't be here for another six minutes. Put your bags down there and I'll keep an eye on them for you.'

Walking home past the drapers, the chemist with yellow cellophaned windows, Mrs Cheyney's General Stores with sacks of sugar and flour just inside the door (and a lethal looking bacon slicer with which it was rumoured the rarely-seen Mr Cheyney carved up stray cats and dogs); then down the long straight path that bisected the green swathe of park, skirted the bowling green, tennis courts and summer house and finally narrowed into what was almost a tunnel, courtesy of the tall beetling privets either side. Our house was down a long avenue latticed with leaves and light. A huge wooden gate, like a stockade, fronted it. Both my younger brother and me, one astride the top and the other pushing, were needed to get it to swing open wide and full. Then, with the pusher clinging on, crab-like, we rode a pirate ship backwards and forwards across the sea of our imaginations.

The 'trippers' arrived on coaches at the other side. They were corralled into camps and only occasionally would we see them on our territory, pedalling two-seater fun bikes, wearing silly hats and chewing gum or smoking. Everyone knew they came from bad areas in Liverpool where there was no fresh air or good food. I saw that the children had grubby mouths and greyish vests and socks, that the women were large and frowsy and that the men had tattoos and drank a lot. Often at night we'd hear the clanging police bells in the distance and my mother would get up and close the French windows with a disapproving shake of her head. They were the sort who ate chips from newspapers and bought cheap gifts on the seafront – plastic windmills, bucket-and-spade sets, lilos in garish pink and orange. The men drank beer from straight glasses rather than the dimpled tankards my father and his friends liked, and the women bought tea in heavy white cups to take down to the beach on a tray, in return for a small deposit.

The summer before my twelfth birthday, 1959, was long and hot. My father was away on an extended business trip all August and without his presence my mother fluttered around the house like a moth distracted by different lights. I was restless and just starting to chafe against the clear and rigid boundaries that had always been in place for me. I was a child who'd been brought up to believe there were two sides to every question: the right and the wrong side. We were right. Morally. Politically. Absolutely. God, The Queen Mother and anyone else who mattered was, without any doubt, on our side. I'd always visualised these convictions as a breakwater keeping any turbulence outside the relatively calm harbour of our everyday lives. But now, with the faint stirrings of adolescence, I found myself on occasions wanting to test the bulwark's strength. On this particular day, when I'd fallen out with my brother and been told off, I craved a small act of revenge. I wanted to do wrong. As it was wrong to go to the other side of the island where we did not belong and unspecified dangers lurked, that is where I would go. I had vague notions of an adventure of my favourite Enid Blyton sort in which jolly exciting scrapes involving robbers, buried treasure and secret hideouts would inevitably play a part.

After lunch, while my brother was having his rest and my mother was on the phone, I indicated that I was going for a walk and swiftly made my way down to the sea front. There I caught a red open-topped bus and rode upstairs at the front, resting my burning face against the coolness of the metal safety bar and pretending that it went wherever I wanted it to. It was as if I was invisible for miraculously the conductor never came to ask for my fare, although I'd been holding the pennies so tightly in my sweaty palm that they left their imprint for the rest of the day. We went past the funfair at the end of the front and it was strange to look down on the rides; the dodgems looked like some kind of exotic beetle, scuttling around with antennae sparking, and the striped tops of the roundabouts revolved like twizzled parasols. As we went further inland and away from the area I knew, the road seemed to get dustier and more uneven, the bungalows and shops straggled then disappeared and the pavement became footpath then just sandy verge. The grit whipped up into my eyes, making them sore, and I lost my headband when a sudden gust of wind buffeted the bus. About ten minutes later we stopped at what were obviously the gates of the holiday camp. A large peeling yellow board proclaimed 'Happy Holiday Village', under which vandals had spray-painted some words which I somehow knew to be rude whilst being unsure of their precise meaning. Having got off the bus along with everyone else, I didn't have to decide what to do next as I found myself swept along with the families who were pouring through the camp gates like molten lava.

Inside I was amazed to find a microcosm of a small town with its own roads, shops and pubs. This was the hub of the camp. Lines of double-deckered chalets, flagged with striped towels and bathing costumes, were spokes which radiated from this centre. Throngs of people, some of whom I seemed to recognise from the front, some of whom I didn't, strolled about noisily yet good-naturedly. There was a welter of colour and texture to everything I saw and heard. Shouts. Laughter. Chatter.

'Bloody 'ell, our Chrissie, will yer just flaming well sherrup. Yer never stop you don't!'

'Throw it over 'ere! 'Ere!'

'I said to him, alright then, if you must. But don't come to me crying about it later...'

'What time is it Jack? What sitting are we on for us tea?'

'Now then, lovey, watch where you're going! Had a nice trip?'

'You're rotten, you are! The little lass 'as cut her leg. You okay, lovey? Ooh, look at those lovely white socks all mucky. What will your Mam say, eh? Let's get you sorted out.'

The buckle on my sandal had broken, and I'd fallen and grazed my knee. It wasn't much but strange hands pulled me up, brushed the worst of the dirt off my dress, complained about the unevenness of the ground and, once they'd assured themselves I was alright, reabsorbed me back into their midst. I wandered about freely, fascinated by the amusement arcades, the steam engine (a mini replica of our own 'Puffing Billy' which pulled trucks of campers around the site), an American donut-making machine, the swimming pool (beside which a hoola-hoop competition was taking place) and the large smoke-filled caverns from which rolled waves of noise and beer fumes. I was hot, sticky and dusty but oblivious to time passing. Coming upon an ice-cream kiosk I decided to buy a Mivvi with my pennies; another small act of rebellion, as my brother and I were only allowed to have ice-cream cornets from the local dairy because my mother knew the people that ran it. I queued up, got my lolly and was just removing its wrapper when a girl, a year or two younger than me, came up and asked for a bite in return for a couple of her chips. I looked down at the greaseproof paper bag wrapped in newspaper. The chips, fat and golden, glistened with vinegar and smelt delicious. More forbidden fruits. Greedily I complied, but as we were completing our swap the girl was cuffed lightly on the back of the head by a woman about my mother's age.

'Maureen! Manners, if you please! It is simply not hygienic to do that sort of thing. If you want a lolly, then just ask me or your dad nicely.'

'Sorry, Mum.'

'And who might this be?'

'Dunno.'

The girl grinned and looked questioningly at me. I shrugged

and avoided her glance, reluctant to sacrifice my anonymity.

'Well, I'm sure whoever's in charge of you would say the same thing. I'm not trying to suggest you've got any terrible disease but it's best to be on the safe side. You get all sorts of people 'ere.'

I had been screwing my eyes up against the light as she spoke, but suddenly the sun went behind a cloud revealing a strikingly attractive woman. Rather like Audrey Hepburn, she had a clear, slightly olive skin, dark hair swept into some kind of arrangement on top of her head and wonderful almond-shaped eyes. The voice was a shock. The accent was what my mother called 'common', but she used it proudly, almost disdainfully and I experienced an acute sense of dislocation.

'Are we going to go over to the dancing competition now, Mo?'

'Yes, Mam.'

'Say goodbye to your little friend then. Perhaps you'll see her later on. Bye, love. Oh, 'ere, have this hanky to clean yourself up with and here's a tanner for some chips of your own.'

She threw me a funny kind of look – embarrassed, kindly, pitying – as she proffered the coin and Kleenex and then firmly ushered Maureen away. I stood there, ineffectually dabbing at the red stickiness around my mouth and chin and feeling suddenly quite sick. I dropped the sixpence onto the ground as if it were infected.

I walked home. Rarely using buses, I'd forgotten I would need the return fare. By the time I reached the front it was early evening and although darkness was still a long time away, fairy lights on some of the stalls were already lit. There weren't many people around; the rides were only half-full and those running them looked bored, taking money woodenly like half-wound-up toys. The music ground on discordantly and some rubbish from a bin blew against my bare legs. I now wanted to be home, whatever trouble was awaiting me, so I hurried on, deciding to take the shortcut through the park. Its familiarity was comforting. There were the swings and roundabout my brother and I had played on ever since I could remember anything, the summer house where last June I'd had my first kiss from James Prindle, and over there the rose gardens where we used to come to do Nature Study with the nursery school. But most importantly, home was just the other end of the tunnelled path. I was really hurrying now, trying in vain to brush from my mind the shadows of the afternoon, the sense that I was standing on shifting sands.

A man stepped out of the shadows in front of me. He didn't look dangerous; he certainly didn't wear a grubby old mac or leer at me like the men about whom we girls had been warned at school. He looked, well, just ordinary – like one of my father's friends, one of the men at the station, in the shops, or any of the men I knew. I think he asked me the time or something like that, I can't quite remember. I muttered a reply and made as if to walk round him; he stepped sideways to block my path and then, holding my left arm, reached forward, drew up my dress and slid his other hand in between my legs, turning his face aside so I couldn't see his eyes. For a brief moment I froze, feeling his dreadful fingers crawl against my flesh; then I pushed at him, hard, and he staggered, letting go his grip, and I ran. Within seconds I was out of the tunnel and flying down the avenue. Our gate was open and, once on the right side, I shoved my shoulder against it and heaved it firmly shut.

I was sent to bed as soon as I got in. My mother was not as angry as she might have been because she'd just heard from my father that he'd be home at the end of the week. She said there was no real harm done. She and my brother were watching a comedy show on the television, 'Charlie Drake' – he kept sneaking up behind these girls and pinching their bottoms. Upstairs, I could hear bursts of high-pitched laughter blare from the set. Curling up between my cotton sheets, I felt the place between my legs moist and I tasted copper, salt and tears on my hands. I slipped into sleep, rocking myself to and fro, backwards and forwards, on the gate between then and now. I'd had my adventure. I'd been to the other side and returned safely back home.

The horror was that I knew the journey could not be unmade and that nothing could ever be safe again.

# Holding Your Breath

Her novelty value hadn't completely worn off. She was still occasionally stopped in the mall and asked to say 'See you later, alligator' by large ladies in Bermuda shorts and bright, baggy T-shirts. When she'd obliged they would say 'You are so cute!' or 'Can you say it again, honey?' or 'Hey Ted! Come and listen to this dear little English girl.'

Some of Sarah's classmates, the nicer ones, would quiz her about the Royal Family as if she was personal friends with them, when in fact the limit of her experience was watching the changing of the guard at Buckingham Palace on a school trip. The worst was Louisa, chubby and with a mouth full of braces, who was in love with Prince Charles. A photo of him was Scotch-taped inside her locker and she sang *Charlie is my darling* when they were getting ready for Physical Recreation. She planned to marry Charles when she was older and regarded Sarah as her own personal instruction manual for helping her achieve this ambition: how to make a pot of tea, how many shillings were in a pound, what it was like to drive on the wrong side of the road, how to deal with fog, rain and no sunshine and when and where to wear a kilt were just some of the answers Sarah dutifully supplied. When she didn't know an answer, such as how much Charles would earn when he was king, she simply made something up and this seemed to keep Louisa happy.

To try and start up conversations Sarah would ask about

President Kennedy and try and look interested when the girls talked about how cute John and Caroline were but her enquiries sounded false even to herself. Sam Hardiston had what he claimed was a piece of the mat that the President had stood on during his inauguration. He kept it in a small plastic bag and charged a dime to touch it. But when Sarah offered him her money he said it was only for Americans to do and that if he let anyone have contact with it who didn't pledge allegiance to the Stars and Stripes both he and that person would go straight to hell. When it was time for the pledge Sarah always stood behind her desk the same as the rest of them but at attention, like for 'God Save the Queen', rather than placing her hand over her heart.

In the schoolyard at recreation, groups of girls would hunch together over dog-eared copies of *Life* looking at pictures of Jackie and admiring all her pretty outfits: the pastel coloured suits with box jackets and the jaunty little pill-box hats. Once there was a picture of the Queen on the cover and they called Sarah over to ask her opinion. The Queen (or Busy Lizzie as Daddy called her) was in a leopard print coat and hat which even Sarah, with her limited fashion sense, knew was dreadful. However, national pride compelled her to say the Queen looked wonderful, and this produced a volley of sniggers from her classmates.

But mostly Sarah was politely ignored and, although in many ways that suited her fine, she felt like a discarded toy, one of those where paint starts rubbing off almost as soon as you've got it home and which before long stops working altogether. Home. It was a word she turned over in her mind a lot. In the early days if Mummy said something like 'It's time to go home now' for a split second she thought it meant they were sailing back to the UK and her heart would jolt with excitement. Home was not London, as everyone seemed to presume, but Cornwall, as far removed from life in

Washington DC as could be (the DC was important as it made sure you weren't confusing it with Washington the state which was thousands of miles away). But after two years in the US of A (as Daddy called it in that fake American accent he thought was so funny) home was beginning to feel unreal, like somewhere in a dream. Shreds of memory would drift into that space inside her head just before she fell asleep or woke up: a ragged coastline, the yellowy burr of Nana Weston's voice like the clotted cream she always served, windy roads with hedges on either side so high that it was like being in a maze, chunks of peppery potato falling out of a pasty, hot Ribena for elevenses with *Workers Playtime* on the radio, Clarks sandals, her copy of *Bunty* flopping through the letterbox every Tuesday with its wonderful smell of damp newsprint.

In Washington DC she went to a public school, which was the opposite of what that meant at home. The school was very big and noisy and she woke every morning completely terrified at the prospect of going there. Her parents sensed something was wrong and gently but firmly questioned her; Sarah forced a smile – one that hurt because you had to concentrate so hard on keeping the muscles in the right position – and insisted that everything was fine. For one thing nothing bad was actually happening to her. She wasn't being hit or picked on or even teased. Well, only a little bit. How could she tell them that she just had this vague sense that something menacing was lurking under the surface of apparent normality. That she was being threatened, though she didn't know how or why.

At home she'd been chatty in school, in fact often too chatty. One end of term report had said she was verbose and she'd thought that was a good thing until she looked the word up in a dictionary. Now speaking became a minefield because she was constantly afraid of using the wrong word. Just the thought of the time when she didn't know that a period was a full-stop made her blush, even if she was by herself, but there were so many other potential causes of embarrassment: admiring a girl's fringe instead of her bangs, asking for crisps when it should be chips, walking on the pavement instead of sidewalk, eating lunch instead of dinner. The list was endless and it was safer to stay quiet. Not only that but she never seemed to wear the right thing either. Back home there'd been a school uniform so you couldn't go wrong. Here you had to make a choice and every morning she went through an agony of indecision about which skirt and top to put on. Each time she got it wrong. Her clothes seemed drab, her shoes flat and plain. The other girls wore pedal pushers and sneakers, chewed gum (which she wasn't allowed to do) and some of them even wore make-up.

They'd already bought her uniform for the grammar school before they knew about the overseas posting. Mummy and her went into Truro one Saturday and bought everything on the long list: navy blue gymslip, two white shirts, tie, a blazer with the school's red and gold crest on the breast pocket, two hats, a velour one for winter and a boater for summer, divided skirt and Aertex shirts for sports, two pairs of hockey socks, hockey boots and a raincoat. The crowning glory was a huge satchel, conker brown, which was not on the list but which Mummy bought her anyway, somehow knowing, without Sarah having said anything, that it had been an object of desire all through her last year at primary school. At least twice a week Sarah would lay everything carefully out on her bed and thrill at the thought of putting it on come September. When the news came through about going to The States it took a while to sink in that she wouldn't actually be going to the grammar school and would never wear the fabulous uniform. Because the price labels hadn't been taken off, the shop agreed to take everything back; Mummy was delighted while Sarah successfully hid her devastation. She kept the satchel, though, and had even taken it to her new school on the first day, but the funny looks she got meant it was shoved into the back of her wardrobe, or closet, as soon as she got home.

The other reason she never said anything was that she didn't want to spoil Mummy and Daddy's happiness. Daddy's job, three years working at the Pentagon, an enormous white building in a funny shape, had transformed their lives, especially Mummy's. In Cornwall she'd obviously been bored and unhappy. Sarah would come home from school to find her sitting on the window seat, smoking and reading a book or sometimes just gazing out to sea. Often the beds weren't even made and there was nothing in the oven for supper when Daddy came home from work. Not that he ever got cross, he just sighed and helped straighten up things. Her parents hardly ever went out, the monthly dinner in the officers' mess being the highlight of their social calendar. Now there were Embassy parties and BBQs and swimming parties at diplomats' houses where there were servants with black faces. During the summer there'd been a camping holiday in Maine and a trip to the Everglades in Florida where they'd seen real live crocs. Mummy sparkled now. She was like a dusty old mirror that had been polished and now reflected light from all angles. She bought lots of new clothes, sang while she tried them on and kissed and hugged Daddy a lot more than she ever used to.

In September Sarah had hoped that the start of a new term – or rather semester – would improve matters. It had been awkward starting in the June: there had been no time to make friends and then there had followed the long, lonely summer break. Now at least she now knew her way round the place and how things worked. In fact, if it hadn't been for the camp the whole thing might have been tolerable. One morning about two weeks after they'd returned her class teacher, Miss Stephens, announced that there would be a two week residential camp in early November. They would be staying in log cabins in the Vermont mountains doing things like rock climbing and survival skills. The whole class was expected to go because it was all about team building and working together as a group. At first Sarah was not worried, assuming that she would not be the only one to whom the prospect of going away to camp was awful beyond words.

However, as it turned out almost all of the class were going. Bobby Walters couldn't because he had kidney disease and so had to stay near a hospital, and Alicia Montgomery looked after her crippled mother, but apart from those two everyone else except Sarah had returned their permission slips and paid their deposit. The thought of the camp made her feel ill with anxiety. Not only did she dislike any outdoor stuff anyway but the opportunities for messing up big time, by saying or doing the wrong thing, were almost limitless. She'd be even further away from home, not just real home in England but the temporary one here, and she'd have to sleep, eat and go to the toilet with a load of kids who basically she didn't trust. Even Louisa could be mean sometimes. Just the other day she'd said deliberately loudly, so Sarah could hear, that England could never have won the war without the help of the Americans.

There'd been whispered talk of illicit activities during the night – raids and initiation rituals – and it was all Sarah could do not to be physically sick. She felt sure this would be used as an excuse to have a real go at her. The teachers couldn't be there all of the time and she would be exposed, vulnerable, to anything they might decide to do. For a couple of weeks now Miss Stephens had been asking for the forms and Sarah had used varying excuses and delaying tactics. She was now in the dangerous position of drawing more attention to herself by not going than going. In desperation she decided to pluck up the courage to speak to her parents that night after supper.

'How's school, darling?' asked Daddy, the same as he did

every time the three of them sat down to eat. He usually pulled her chair out with a flourish, as if he was a waiter in a posh restaurant, but he didn't this time. Instead he sat down heavily, looking serious and distracted.

'It's OK,' Sarah said, 'the thing is, though...'

'Don't say OK,' Mummy said, spooning vegetables onto an already full plate. 'It's sloppy speech. Heaven help us if you go back talking completely in Americanisms.'

'She can't be blamed for picking up some of the idioms.' Daddy snapped. 'Anyway, it hardly matters now does it?'

'Of course it matters!'

'For God's sake, can I have some meat with that or am I expected to survive just on peas and carrots?'

'Damn you! Serve yourself then!' and with that Mummy burst into tears and rushed out of the room, holding her apron up to her eyes.

Sarah sat rigid with fear. Her parents sometimes bickered with one another but it normally followed a familiar pattern on well-worn subjects such as her father's untidiness or her mother's extravagance, and it had never given her any cause for concern. This was different: a tension which she was dimly aware had been thrumming in the air for a couple of weeks now. There had been discussions in low voices which stopped suddenly if she entered the room; one morning she had come down to breakfast and found her parents huddled round the radio. More often than not now Daddy went back to the office after supper to do more work. She wondered if her parents were going to divorce. Several of her classmates had divorced parents, although Sarah could not remember any at her old school back home.

Perhaps if she was away they could work it out. Maybe they were worried about her and that had been adding to the pressure. In silence Sarah went to her school bag and produced the information pack about the camp and the permission forms. Daddy read everything, signed the forms and then wrote a cheque for a large amount of dollars without even questioning the amount like he usually did. With a heavy heart, Sarah handed the paperwork in to Miss Stephens the following morning. Her fate was sealed.

It was October and Sarah was missing the damp, cosy Autumn of home. Why did the U S of A (Daddy no longer said that or anything else in a funny voice now) insist on having everything bigger? Their trees were bigger and the trees had more leaves turning more shades of russet, gold and brown. At home it would be Bonfire Night in November but here, she'd been told, there would only be some stupid Thanksgiving celebration later that month, though giving thanks for what she didn't know and didn't care. She kicked at the leaves as she walked, wondering if perhaps at camp she should arm herself with something just in case. A kitchen knife was the only weapon she would be able to get hold of but just the thought of a blade coming into contact with skin made her shudder. Mind you, she wouldn't ever use the thing. It would just be there to warn anybody off. Would she be able to hide a knife in her case when she went away? Mummy normally insisted on packing her things but she hadn't been concentrating much for the last couple of weeks – in fact she was back to being a dusty mirror – so maybe she'd get away with it.

The first surprise came when she arrived at school. Back in England they'd had assemblies where the headmaster read out notices, but here the school was too big for that, so they had a tannoy system which the Principal used on the very rare occasions when he needed to speak to all of the pupils, or rather students. This was one of those times. After the pledge, Miss Stephens asked them all to sit quietly, and soon the Principal's voice crackled through the speakers like gunfire making some of the girls scream in mock fright and the boys jeer at them. By the time Miss Stephens had quietened everyone down the Principal was well into his address, but the sound quality was poor and, sitting at the back, Sarah could only make out odd phrases. Not that she was concentrating much, anyway, being busy calculating what were the minimum number of hours of sleep she could survive on while at camp so as to be awake and vigilant in case of attack.

Gradually she became aware that the atmosphere in the room had changed. It wasn't only that you could have heard a pin drop; jaws had stopped working, fingers had stopped drumming on the desktops, feet were placed squarely on the floor. But glancing around she saw that her classmates, usually so big and brash, seemed suddenly to have shrunk: they were younger, less colourful and somehow not as much a natural part of their surroundings as she'd always thought. They can be scared too, she realised with a jolt, and for the first time since she'd arrived in this strange, alien land Sarah experienced a wisp of empathy with those around her.

Words floated into the room and settled like dust motes.

Nuclear attack.

Khrushchev.

Missiles.

Louisa started to cry quietly but nobody shushed her. The thick, red neck of the boy in front of Sarah was beaded with sweat. Through the window she could see an airplane scratching the surface of the clear blue sky and she wondered whether it was bringing people into the country or taking them out. The Principal had stopped talking and now Miss Stephens was speaking. Even she looked diminished by what was happening. Ashen-faced, she clutched the edge of her desk for support and told them, with just the faintest wobble in her voice, not to be afraid and that the United States of America was a good and powerful country and that the Russians would not bully them.

Sarah knew something about politics. She'd heard Daddy say *Better dead than Red* and knew that Russia was their enemy. The Russians in charge wore big fur coats and hats and never smiled, and if someone in their country had a different opinion to the people in charge they were sent to prison camps in Siberia. It was the Russians who'd put a big wall up in the middle of Berlin which split the city into two so that the Communists in the Eastern bit couldn't escape and have a nice life in the West. This was called the Iron Curtain even though it wasn't a curtain. There were gun turrets on top of the wall and anyone who tried to cross over it got shot dead.

How Cuba came to be a part of this was more complicated, but over the next few days Sarah managed to sift some facts from the avalanche of increasingly bizarre rumours that swamped the school. It seemed that the Russians had put some missiles on Cuba and had pointed them directly at Washington DC. The Americans demanded that they be removed and the Russians said no and so it was very likely that the two countries would drop nuclear bombs on one another and this would be the end of the world. Over the next week at school all the teachers and students regularly trooped down into the basements and crouched with their backs against the walls and their arms shielding their heads. Sarah couldn't see the point of this, given what she knew radiation could do, but she was happy to be doing the same as everyone else, especially when on the second occasion the sirens sounded Louisa reached for her hand. Because of Daddy's job in the Pentagon she was bombarded with questions about what was happening, and every morning and every recreation a knot of girls and boys would be gathered round her desk hanging on her every word. Not that she could offer them much. Daddy was rarely at home, and when she did see him his face was grey and etched with tiredness. He didn't crack jokes anymore and had taken to scooping her up and hugging her so tightly that it hurt. Every day Mummy went to the supermarket and bought as many tinned goods as she could, though the shelves were fast emptying because of panic buying. Sarah helped stack them into the back of their station wagon.

Mummy and Daddy were always sneaking off to have urgent conversations that often ended with Mummy crying and saying that she wanted to go home, which should have made Sarah feel good but it didn't. One day her parents had a really bad row because Mummy was ringing her parents every day and calls cost a pound a minute. Daddy said she would ruin them and Mummy screamed back that as they were all going to die anyway what did it matter.

On Tuesday 24th October Sam Hardiston said that if a Russian ship shot across the bows of an American ship that would mean war was declared. Someone else said that if the missiles weren't disabled by midday on the dot then that meant war was declared. As midday approached a lot of girls became hysterical and had to be taken to the medical centre. But midday came and went and after that, although rumours still surfaced they seemed to have lost their force, like when a big storm is dying down but you still get eddies of wind swirling around.

When the inevitable cancellation of the camp was announced, Sarah surprised herself by experiencing a twinge of disappointment. Ironically, Vermont was the place chosen by the Embassy for an evacuation of British citizens which in the end never happened. However, the fact that she and her family would have been afforded preferential treatment along with the vague assumption, not challenged by Sarah, that her father had played some part in the resolution of the crisis secured her position within the class. The following month she spent Thanksgiving weekend at Louisa's and at Christmas she was elected as her class's representative on the Student Council. When, years later, she read that the world held its breath for those thirteen days in 1962, all Sarah could remember clearly about that brief period in her life was at last feeling able to breathe more easily.

# A True Vocation

It was not until his late forties that Richard discovered his true vocation. Even his doting mother, Lady Faresham, who had always insisted upon him being a 'late developer' had begun to lose patience, while his father Admiral 'Snorty' Faresham had never had any in the first place. Their only son had been given the best start in life that money could buy – exclusive prep school, renowned public school and a junior partnership in The City. Richard had not been an out-and-out failure – there would have been some glory in that – he had simply not been a success. Lack of physical co-ordination on the sports field and lack of mental co-ordination in the classroom had ensured no honours at school; however a pleasant and co-operative manner did ensure that he drew no attention to himself. He was someone his peer group considered neither worth bullying or befriending. For two years running he was left off the form lists completely and while some boys in time-honoured fashion appeared twice in the school photo, he didn't appear at all.

Fading away from school into the job in the City was a painless transition but a similarly undistinguished move. He didn't make any spectacular mismanagements but neither did he land any new contracts. However, with the recession hitting an all-time low even his father's influence couldn't prevent him from being made redundant. Richard cleared his desk of his few possessions, bid colleagues farewell without rancour and returned home to the alternate roaring and bleating of his father and mother. Shrugging his shoulders, thereby successfully evading the hurled candelabra, he good-naturedly signed on at the local unemployment office, and during the course of the next seven months was variously a window cleaner, a pizza delivery man, a brickie and a hospital orderly, while his parents pretended to friends that he was engaged in charity work. He did his best – all his employers concurred on that point – it was just that his best resulted in a certain degree of mayhem. Mind you, as he explained to his unemployment officer, it was just a lucky coincidence that when he was doing his hospital job he was able to take down to theatre the chap whose toes he had broken when he'd dropped the hod on the building site.

Then he became a vicar. The Bishop had been round for tea one day, and in the course of him bemoaning the lack of young men entering the ministry and his mother bemoaning Richard's lack of purpose in life, some sort of decision had been reached, to be later ratified when his father endowed the theological college with a large sum of money in return for them waiving their entry requirements. Richard did attempt to interject that belief in God was one entry requirement he didn't possess, but was sharply told that was irrelevant. There followed three years at college when the Fareshams felt able to hold their heads high once again in the community. 'Our son, the priest,' Lady Faresham would intone, her hands clasped in front of her as if in prayer. She took to visiting the poor and needy, such as those unfortunates who could only afford to run one car, taking baskets of bruised and seeping apples from their orchard which her victims consigned to the bin as soon as she had left.

Richard was assigned to a small, nondescript country parish whose Church Restoration Fund's thermometer of contributions was stuck at 1969. The previous incumbent had been an alcoholic homosexual, neither trait a problem in itself, but the incident with the goat (kept tethered in the graveyard in a futile attempt to keep the grass down) had been rather public, occurring as it did when the bridal party arrived. The police agreed not to press charges on condition there was a swift replacement in the vicarage. The bishop decided Richard was the obvious choice – he had no apparent virtues but no vices either, and within a week the new appointment was effected.

Richard, as ever, tried hard. There were no catastrophes as there had been with his predecessor – no baby's names mixed up at christenings, sermon notes lost, or choir boys fondled. Everyone agreed he was very... well, ordinary, if perhaps somewhat uninspired. Numbers at morning service didn't dwindle (though admittedly this would have been difficult as they averaged three) but didn't rise either. But then something did rise, and it was as unexpected as it was sudden.

Richard had never had a lot to do with women. He had been sheltered from their company throughout his schooling (even Matron was quite obviously a man in disguise) and at work he lacked the social skills to approach them. Indeed, the unfortunate incident while he'd been window cleaning had been due to him failing to recognise the signals being given out by the scantily clad young woman whose leaded lights he was polishing. He was, therefore, no match for the spinsters of the parish who, within hours of his appointment being confirmed, mounted their campaign or, perhaps more accurately, campaigned to be mounted. Invitations to lunch, tea and supper he could handle, more subtle invitations he failed to recognise. Thus it was that Miss Prendle achieved the first victory, in the vestry, her only weapons a generous shot of rum in his coffee and the disclosure of black basque and suspenders worn under her choir robes. It was Miss Prendle who discovered the incredible truth behind the colourless facade that passed for Richard Faresham.

He had found his true vocation, his true calling. It was not just the size of his equipment, the versatility with which he employed it, or his stamina – though all these were incredible.

He found in himself a natural talent for pleasuring each woman – young or old, beautiful or plain – just as they would wish in their wildest fantasies. To his astonishment, he was magnificent at sex, a supreme master of the art as his increasingly large female congregation would testify. Miss Prendle enjoyed missionary position but with handcuffs, whereas Miss Henderson insisted on being on top. With Mrs Durrant, he had to perform on her late husband's gravestone and with Miss Williams to Ravel's *Bolero*. He was delighted to comply with whatever his parishioners wanted and, confident of the power beneath his cassock, so his outward demeanour became more assertive. His sermons became fiery, he strode around the parish rather than ambled and he spoke with conviction to troubled souls and tortured minds. There was a sensuality about his services – the rich throbbing music of the organ, the profusion of fruit and flowers at Harvest time, even the pious scenes depicted in the stained glass windows seemed to be somehow suggestive. When he slowly raised the chalice of communion wine to his lips, one could almost hear a collective sigh escape from the ladies present. Never had so many buns been baked for the Parish coffee mornings, never so many squares knitted for the homeless or carols sung so lustily at Christmas. The Appeal Fund flourished, the thermometer bubbled over and a new Church roof was soon in place. The Parish Hall was renovated, Sunday School classes and Bible study classes were reinstated and the Bishop was delighted.

'Hidden talents, that's what your boy's got, hidden talents!' he pronounced to Admiral and Lady Faresham as they took dry sherry one evening.

'Just knew he had it in him!' boomed the Admiral, sinking another schooner.

'He was always a very spiritual person, even as a child,' purred Lady Faresham. 'It's just taken him a little while to come out of himself.'

As she spoke, Richard had just succeeded in bringing Miss Prendle to her fourth multiple orgasm. 'Oh my God!' she moaned in ecstasy. Richard was a bit worried about the bed in the vicarage. It was creaking rather alarmingly, hardly surprising given the activity it had been subjected to just about every day since he'd moved in.

Richard knew it would all have to end, and the crack in the ceiling provided the sign that he'd been looking for. For one thing, Miss Prendle, Mrs Durrant, Miss Williams and the others were getting very competitive for his attentions. They gave him so many meals that he was becoming increasingly bloated, and for some weeks now he hadn't even been able to see that bit of him the ladies held so dear. Each was confident of being his only sexual partner and Richard found watching his every word and action very carefully a great strain. It all came to a head, so to speak, one Sunday in October when Richard had conducted four services – Matins, Evensong, Mrs Durrant and Miss Henderson. The former liaison had occurred, as always, in the graveyard, but a light frost had fallen and afterwards Richard found himself to be sore and chapped – a clear case of frostbite to the buttocks. Later, bouncing beneath Miss Henderson, the inflamed skin chafed against the sheet and caused him considerable discomfort. Unfortunately, Miss Henderson mistook his cries of pain to be those of pleasure and increased her level of activity. Consummation of the act was out of the question as Richard, now in extreme distress, shut his eyes and for the first time genuinely prayed for help. It came (something of which at that moment he was incapable) in the form of the bed finally giving way to the level of abuse it had suffered and collapsing in a splintering, groaning heap – indeed, not unlike Richard himself.

After Miss Henderson's tearful departure Richard went into the front room and gloomily poured himself a large whisky. Settling himself down in his favourite armchair, having firstly ensured several extra cushions were in place, he took several long swallows of his drink and leant back against the headrest. And there it was – a huge crack in the ceiling, caused by the collapse of the iron bedstead in the room directly above. But not an ordinary meandering purposeless crack; this one knew what it was. One long line bisected by a shorter line about two thirds of the way up its length – it was a cross. Richard spluttered with disbelief and rubbed his eyes, initially blaming the strength of the whisky. But there was no doubt; he had prayed and had been given a sign. His true vocation had been disclosed to him and he phoned the Bishop that same evening.

Given Richard's subsequent career it was perhaps fortunate that Admiral and Lady Faresham were both killed in a car crash the same day. The Admiral failed to negotiate a rather difficult bend on his way back from the Golf Club, where he'd downed considerably more than his usual ration of five G & T's due to it being Raggy Ragglestone's anniversary of something or other. The car hit Lady Faresham, who was just returning from church, and they were both killed instantly. Everyone said what a wonderful funeral it was.

With his inheritance Richard bought a small run-down nightclub in a town not far from his ex-parish, and over the next few months succeeded in transforming it into one of the hottest night spots around. The waitresses were dressed as nuns, the revealing nature of their dress giving the Club its name, 'The Dirty Habit', while the barmen were bare-chested except for dog collars. However, it was the floor show that bought the crowds in, and they were never disappointed. Misses Prendle, Henderson and Williams were the Swinging Spinsters and indeed they made the most of swinging what they had. Mrs Durrant was Widow Whacker and performed her act with an impressive array of whips and canes. The climax of the show was the entrance of Dick the Vic – a slimmed down Richard complete in vicar's vestments which he shed during the course of his act to reveal a gold satin posing pouch, the size of which sent coachloads of hen parties into near mass hysteria. At the end of the show, Richard acknowledged the audience's rapturous response in his characteristic stance of head dropping to one side, arms flung wide apart and legs together with one knee slightly bent.

'Jesus Christ!' breathed one of the onlookers in awe. And indeed that's just who Richard felt he was.

# Two Ophelias and Me

Two of my friends have jumped off the Humber Bridge now, so it's a kind of special place for me. Every time I walk under or over it I wonder exactly where they jumped from, because unless they walked a good quarter of a mile they could well have splatted onto the Clive Sully which would have been just plain messy. Much better to have had the brown waters of the Humber close over them as softly and noiselessly as the curtains did at the crematorium. I like to think of their hair and clothes streaming out like twin Ophelias (the three of us went to see Hamlet once. I thought I wouldn't understand a word and actually I didn't, but it was brilliant all the same) as they drift down deep, deep onto the riverbed.

Lin was large and blonde, deputy head of a local primary school. She wore very loud clothes – pink satin shirts, strappy high-heeled sandals and I remember one flowery two-piece, belted at the waist and fringed at the hem, that made her look rather like one of those overstuffed hanging baskets in which plants struggle for space like people on an packed lifeboat, leaning out over the sides desperate to get breath. There was always a petal-shaped gap between the third and fourth buttons on her blouse because she would never admit she needed a size 18, and anyway was always thinking she'd go on a diet that would transform her into her ideal size 12. Through this gap you could see a flash of lace encasing an orb of flesh that wobbled and shifted as if it was unconnected to the rest of her body. Sometimes her ankles would swell slightly and the flesh would ooze over her little sandals. She did have very small feet, I'll give her that, but everything else was overblown. Her lips were too shiny, her nails too pointed, her earrings too long. Even her handwriting was too big, she signed her name with a huge, fleshy L and on top of the i was a bubble instead of a dot. She *seemed* very confident – it was only when you got to know her you realised how insecure she was. She knew loads of people too – that was why I could never understand why she bothered at all with me.

Lyndsey (I know the names are similar and I did think of changing them to avoid confusion, but I'm afraid that's what they were called) was more of your natural suicidal type. Always depressed was Lyndsey. Thin, pale, she wore long dark clothes and played the sort of music that sounded as though you'd put it on too slow a speed. Talked a lot about the meaning of life, or the lack of it. Not that I ever thought she'd actually go and do it, but with her it was less of a shock. The first time she and Lin met – I asked them both over for a meal – it was a disaster. Not the meal – I did a steak and kidney pud, just like Mam had taught me, for the main course and bought some Häagen-Dazs for afters and it all seemed to go down very well. But the two of them were at daggers drawn all night. Funny, when I thought they'd get on so well. Lin was just too bossy and Lyndsey too miserable. We all got a bit drunk, Lin called Lyndsey 'face ache' and Lyndsey cried so much she was sick over my new duvet cover. We had another couple of jaunts – the Hamlet trip (Lyndsey's idea, she said she could only enjoy tragedy) and to Alton Towers (Lin wanted to try the Wall of Death) – but it never really worked. I always ended up as pig in the middle.

'A rose between two thorns, more like,' Mam said when I told her.

Lyndsey had a lot to cry about – she'd never known her Dad, and her mother had a nervous breakdown when she was only twelve so she had to help her Nanna bring up her two younger brothers. Then she'd finally got away from home to go to University but couldn't hack the course and cracked up just before the second year exams. Her boyfriend, Nick the Prick (her name for him, not mine, he was always okay with me) had then walked out leaving her with a pile of debts. And genital warts. Finally, her Nanna had died which was how I came to know Lyndsey as her Nanna had spent her last few weeks in the Nursing Home where I work. You really had to feel sorry for her. Lin didn't though. Told me later she thought Lyndsey was 'wallowing in it' and why didn't she go out and get a job to take her mind off things. Lyndsey, on the other hand, said why didn't Lin stop stuffing her face unless she liked looking like Mr Blobby. I tried explaining to her that Lyndsey hadn't got a family either in the sense that her folks lived down South and were snobby because she only taught at a primary school rather than at a University like they both did. But it wasn't any use.

Anyway, they both seemed to like talking to me for some reason. I suppose it's because I'm so ordinary, not having an interesting job like Lin's (the stories she used to tell me about the kiddies!) or a terrible past like Lyndsey's. I'm really very dull, ordinary. My job as Care Assistant means I mop up after incontinent old biddies all day which hardly makes for being brilliant company and I have a bedsit just round the corner from my Mam and Dad. I go to them on Wednesday evenings for my tea and take my washing which saves hanging around in the launderette (mind you, that's where I met Lin), which Mam returns to me, ironed and aired, on a Friday. Then the two of us will either go to Bingo or to a film because that's the night Dad goes down to the Legion for a couple of pints. Saturday Mam and I will shop, if I'm not on duty that is, and on a Sunday dinnertime the three of us will sit down for a casserole with fresh veg from Dad's allotment, after we've been to Mass at St. Vincent's. Whit week we go to Butlins at

Skegness and in the summer we just have days out, usually up the coast to Brid or Scarborough, occasionally Whitby.

On these outings I usually leave Mam and Dad in the car and walk. I do like walking. Even though I'm on my feet most of the day, there's nothing like striding out to blow the cobwebs away. Lin would never walk anywhere, she'd squeeze into her Fiat Panda to go to the post-box (which was about 100 yards from her front door) and anyway, she'd never wear suitable footwear. Lyndsey would always complain that her legs ached or she had a migraine if I suggested a walk, so I got used to going by myself. Funnily enough, down on the foreshore looking up at the Bridge was one of my favourite walks. From a distance, I used to wonder how the Bridge could hold up the way it did; how those wires which looked so thin could support it against all the high winds, how those concrete towers that looked like kiddies' building bricks could carry all those heavy loads that went across. When I was up close it seemed massive, like a giant had made it; I seemed so small, and all the cars seemed like toy ones.

Lyndsey jumped first and Lin did it about six weeks later. It sounds awful, I know, but I thought it was like they were both trying to get my attention, trying to outdo each other. People have said to me, *don't you feel strange having two friends killing themselves like that, don't you feel guilty*, and I say no, I don't. Lyndsey told me what she felt like when she got on the scales and she'd put on another two pounds, and she still had a pile of tests to mark, and she thought that no man would ever want to have sex with her because she was so gross. And Lin told me how she felt when some violin concerto made her heart feel as if it was splitting, and she thought of her Mam hitting her head against the wall till it bled while the two little lads watched and wept. And I sympathised, or rather I tried to, because I could never really understand what they did. I'm just not imaginative like that. Don't get me wrong, it makes me very sad to think of L and L. The funerals were terrible and I cried buckets, even more than when Pat died on *EastEnders*. I even stopped going to Mass for a few weeks. I wish they were still here. But the thing is they didn't want to be – just like so many of the old bids I look after every day. The difference is, at least they could choose.

So I keep on with my life, such as it is, and keep on walking. Sometimes Neil (we were at school together and he's training to be a chef) natters to come with me and I say 'alright, you can if you like.' The trouble is he'll always be asking me what I'm thinking, or if I love him, or telling me things I don't want to know like how much in debt the Bridge Board is and how the tolls are likely to go up. And all the time he's talking I'm thinking: what if I could be flying around up there somewhere, and I could swing the wires of the Bridge over and over, faster and faster, until all the cars and lorries are flung into the water, like a Giant playing a cruel skipping game.

Daft, that's what they called me at school. Spent all my time there daydreaming.

Down on the foreshore the river sludges onto the pebbles. Rats live amongst boulders on the crumbling embankments. In the distance you can see the chemical works belching out gases, and often the air is mucky with all the pollution. But when I see Barton on the South Bank and know that I can walk across that incredible Bridge any time I want to, I feel very glad that I'm not clever or complicated, that I'm me.

'That's called being content,' Mam says, when one Sunday teatime I try to tell her and Dad how I feel. 'Content with your lot. Not like those other poor lasses.'

But, I say, what if I carry on walking, don't come back, what if I just leave the commodes and Neil and the routine? Perhaps I could be different to what I am.

'What? Go over yon side and join yellowbellies!' snorts Dad. 'Don't be talking so silly, girl. Here, have another cup of tea.'

And as he passes my cup I notice that his hand has got some liver spots on and it's shaking slightly, like the wires on the Bridge when the wind's up. And I take my cup, and gulp at the tea too quickly and it's too hot, and it's that which makes tears smart in my eyes.

# End of the World

I came to think of the February half-term as an eyesore on the year's landscape. Unlike the October week, from which one looked down on the glittering lights of the festivals, or the May week which sat comfortably in the warm valley between Spring and Summer, it squatted on a piece of waste land; part of Winter but stripped of the latter's seductive camouflage. I saw it as a time when New Year resolutions had long since been buried and hard unbroken earth stretched ahead as far as the eye could see. Already a stunted month, the holiday foreshortened it even further; a time of locked gates, boarded-up shop fronts and 'Open Again at Easter' signs, a closed-down time.

Our second year together, we spent that particular week with friends of yours in a ramshackle cottage at Spurn Point, a long spit of land which narrows and narrows until its tip, like a dragon's tail, curls and dips into the North Sea. 'The End of the World' as you jokingly termed it. Year after year great chunks of shingle and sand were being swallowed up by the sea, I remember you telling me, and eventually the whole Point would become a number of separate islands. I remember you telling me a lot of things – about geography (your subject), teaching, children, politics, life in general. I, younger, coming to the North for the first time into my first teaching job, seemed to know so little. You held me cupped in the palm of your hand and your voice completely filled the space around me like the booming of the waves and the growling of the wind outside the cottage at night. I could not help but listen.

The so-called cottage was little more than a hut with stone floors, an open range and one outside rusted-up tap. It was achingly cold. The front door didn't seal properly and sand blew in even when it was closed. It settled in the food and inside our clothes. But we made light of the hardships, swept and re-swept the floors and rubbed at our gritty eyes until they were puffy and pink. We walked for miles, crouched in reeds waiting to spot and photograph different sea-birds, threw pebbles into the hissing sea and stubbed toes and grazed hands clambering over the wet rocks. At night we cocooned ourselves in sleeping bags, swollen green caterpillars, and only touched fingers before we went to sleep – just like a married couple, you said, and I pretended not to mind, thinking it was enough that we were together. In the same way I pretended not to notice how the lack of warmth or comfort served to emphasise the distance between us, the chasm of ice that gaped increasingly wider. I was a good actress despite being an indifferent Drama teacher. I masked the fact that I preferred hot, steamy, atmospheres – reading in front of a fire, blotching first one, then the other side of my pale flesh or sitting in the corner of a crowded, music-filled pub feeling squeezed of air. That's why the only time I liked school was in winter when the windows had misted up and the smell of bodies hung dank and fetid in the gloom of late afternoon. Sex was best those times when we thrashed about in the coarse sheets of that cheap hotel and afterwards, unable to open the window which had jammed, fugging the room with cigarette smoke. You preferred the outside; I could always smell it on your clothes and in the salty roughness of your beard. You had to look forward, outward, while my instinct was to crawl back and huddle, embryonic, inside myself.

I have some photos. One was taken of the two of us, unawares, as we trudged side by side through the sand-dunes and tall grasses; bent against the wind, our hair and coats streaming behind us. You have your hands deep in your pockets and are gazing directly ahead. My head is slightly turned towards you and a strand of hair has whipped across my face. I have another one of you, alone, on the shore-line holding a piece of white driftwood like a huge bleached bone; behind you the backcloth of grey sea and sky is seamless. And there's one of me, perched on a rusty oil-drum, determinedly smiling to the camera, only later noticing the brown marks like old blood-stains on the seat of my clothing. Later, I would scrutinise these photos minutely for signs, expressions, signals that I had failed to notice at the time.

You went back to your wife shortly afterwards and I wasn't really surprised. At least you never pretended, either to her or to me, to be anything other than you were, although I hadn't realised I was not the first to have been taken to the Point to mark the final act of the play. That element of stage management in what had appeared so natural did hurt, hurt badly. I decided to expose my wounds to the open air rather than binding them tightly with layers of self-deception as I'd always done before. They were raw and they stung, especially that time I met the two of you with the children all out shopping together, or when I noticed you talking to my replacement in the staffroom while she looked up at you in a way that was so familiar it was like holding up a magnifying glass to my pain.

I left at the end of the summer term and for the first time in my life felt as though I had stopped trying to follow timetables that had been devised by others. For the moment, there was no future and the concept of time became meaningless. I tore up the calendar and carefully packed away my clocks, wristwatch and diary. I lived in the present, which was as short or long as that particular second, minute, hour or day seemed to be. Sometimes I would pick at the scabs of my resentment, making them bleed afresh, but of course, in time, they did heal and the seal of new skin was tougher than before. February passed almost without my noticing it.

In the Spring I arranged to stay in the cottage once more, this time by myself. It was still as bleak and cold as I'd remembered but by then it didn't matter. I'd adapted, both in the practical sense by bringing with me draught excluders, heaters, a stove, extra blankets and clothing and within myself too. At last, I could distinguish between what was really me and what was external and maintain some kind of balance. You were wrong, you see, wrong about so many things, not least about mentally dividing up time and yourself. Both are too precious, too much of a complex intricately-worked mosaic, to be hacked into pieces. The important thing to do is to live in the moment, not outside it. Time will just flow on regardless, like the water round the Point, so you might as well be swept along together. And you were mistaken about Spurn – it is being eroded but it reforms itself too – certainly it will never break up into the archipelago of your imagination.

It and I will both survive. In fact, if you walk along the shore in the early morning you can just about see the South Bank when the shroud of mist lifts. It doesn't feel like the end of the world anymore – more like the beginning.

*Enjoy!*

# VALLEY PRESS

Independent literary publishing in
Scarborough, North Yorkshire since 2008

www.valleypressuk.com

Valley Press, Woodend, The Crescent,
Scarborough, YO11 2PW

jamie@valleypressuk.com

Enjoy!

# Paper Flowers

The prison stood on a long, straight characterless road which ran alongside the estuary, past the now-neglected docks and through a hinterland of abandoned warehouses, patches of windswept wasteland and boarded-up shops. As she got off the bus, the image that always struck her was that of the giant's castle in her nightmares as a child: the towering grey mass scraping against a grey canopy of sky, the rows of barred slits behind which she felt hundreds of hungry eyes devour her as she waited to cross the busy road; and looming ahead the huge wooden and iron gate which periodically slid open as if by magic to admit a police van, coach or delivery truck. The spiky whorls of barbed wire which spiralled along the tops of the unbroken flanks of brick were dragon's trails. The diesel fumes and dust whipped up by the continuous stream of heavy traffic swirled around her feet like the mist of dreams.

Yet the flowers that bloomed in the beds at the front of the prison were real enough – polyanthus, crocuses and tulips in tarty reds, oranges, purples and yellows, small daubs of colour in an otherwise rinsed-out land and seascape. They never failed to lighten her spirit as she approached the main entrance. Who tended them she didn't know. Maybe a trusted prisoner or a gardener, though she'd never seen anyone at work. It was as if they flourished to spite their grim environment and, although it was not a metaphor she had ever consciously articulated, they represented to her the freedom of the spirit, the refusal to be cowed that she'd encountered so often inside the walls. She was aware that this could be seen as naivety, a simplistic belief in the goodness of humanity that was perhaps particularly unsuited to her job as a prison teacher. She'd seen the look behind the eyes of some of the prison officers, the look that belied the pleasantries they exchanged with her, the look that said she was another silly middle-class bitch, coming in to this human muck-heap with her paper qualifications and paper ideals. To some extent she could appreciate their tacit disdain, knowing that the education she held out to the inmates as a possible escape for them was, for her and for so many like her, not a question of facts, figures and theories ingested and absorbed but part of her being, her membership of an overworld determined prenatally. Yet at the same time she could not give up her belief in the potential of education to transform and liberate. She returned their gaze defiantly.

She arrived at the entrance, pressed the buzzer and gave her name and identification number through the intercom. Instead of receiving the usual curt acknowledgement followed by the opening of the door, she was told to wait. It was April and the air and ground were hard. She was cold. Sheltering in the lee of the wall she watched as, with each suck and blow of wind that came from passing lorries, the flowers arched their slender stems over as if they must break and then struggled back upright. She huddled further into her duffle coat, pushing her hands deep into its pockets, and again fingered the folded pieces of foolscap that Connors had pushed at her at the end of the previous class. Since then she had read and reread their contents with mounting excitement. It was the breakthrough for which she had waited. To an outsider it might read like nothing more than a lucid, above average A-level literature essay. But she saw it as so much more. Connors had finally succeeded in casting himself free from the subjective, often idiosyncratic, perspective which had anchored him to his background, his origins, with such deadening effect.

She started and involuntarily gripped the pieces of paper as a seagull rose and curved, screeching, across the blank canvas of the grey sky. With Connors' latest bit of work it was as if finally his intellect and imaginative perception had been able to soar above the seemingly hopeless facts of his situation.

He was one of four in an English class that had originally numbered twelve. Serving ten years for armed robbery, he had first come to her two years ago with no aim beyond that of getting out of his cell for a few hours a week. She could now gently tease him about those first few months when he sat at the back of the room, arms tightly folded across his body like a bud afraid of frost, face expressionless, grudgingly producing a few lines of writing in his tiny cramped style. But somehow he'd managed to remain there amid the flux of prison life; his handwriting had become loose and sprawling and the small smelly classroom appeared to shrink as his gestures, voice and presence grew. He became a thirsty student, easily bored, passing quick judgements and demanding from her increasingly sophisticated reading matter. Through literature he sloughed off the dead skin of his past life and through his responses, like a two-way mirror, she saw reflected back certain aspects of herself. At times it distorted that self-image which she so cherished and for which she had worked so hard; that of someone rich in experiences, someone who had seen Life. Still single in her late thirties, she'd travelled and read widely and was in the process of writing her second novel, which took as its theme inner city deprivation and its effects on the working-class community. Free-wheeling in relationships and jobs, never offering full commitment to either, she had succeeded, she would frequently say, in liberating herself from both the shackles of domesticity and career ambition.

They'd spent the last week looking at T.S. Eliot's *The Wasteland*. She'd extracted the main themes and sketched them out for him in her usual clear-sighted way. He stopped her in mid-sentence as she elaborated on the way Eliot used the Great European Tradition to underpin his work.

'That's a load of shit,' he pronounced. There was no anger in his voice, just a complete and utter certainty.

She challenged him with raised eyebrows.

'This poem isn't about tradition, it's about now. It's about *out there*, where there won't be nothing worth getting out for if we're not careful. It's about despair.'

'What evidence is there in the text that...' she began.

He leaned forward over the table, his knuckles clenched white, the tattoos on the back of his hands spreading like a web over the taut skin.

'Despair, that's what this Eliot fella's on about. I know. Stop pretending you do.'

Looking at her watch she frowned in irritation. Ten minutes late. Possibly a cell search going on. Her feet felt damp and chilled. She started to walk to and fro under the shadow of the huge wall. She was impatient to complete the tedious and time-consuming business of being admitted into the prison and making her way through it; of reaching the education block and signing herself in, checking materials out and liaising with duty officers over names and numbers until finally the door to the classroom could be closed and they could re-immerse themselves in the immediacy of the printed word. She walked more briskly now, feeling restricted, constrained, experiencing a sensation of tightness in her chest. The urge to introduce Connors to the idea of an Open University degree was strong but she knew the timing had to be right. She had nurtured him carefully, with delicacy, but it was important that she didn't pre-empt his own sense of readiness for the next stage.

She stopped by the flowers, put down her bag of books and

took out her old battered copy of *Othello*, the text on which they had just begun work. Frowning in concentration, she leafed through the book for a reference she needed but had been unable to find the previous evening. She and Connors had been arguing about the nature of evil. He saw the play in political terms, as a class struggle, with Iago's role as that of revolutionary. While not being out of sympathy with his general thesis, she had accused him of an interpretation which allowed Iago to be absolved of personal responsibility. Then she found the lines for which she'd been searching – so near the beginning of the play that she had overlooked them.

> *'Tis in ourselves*
> *that we are thus or thus. Our bodies are our*
> *gardens to the which our wills are gardeners;*

She looked up, irritated because she had foolishly not remembered the words as spoken by Iago. She snapped the book shut and bent down to replace it in her bag, then crouched there for a few moments chafing her cold hands. She peered at the flowers, suddenly disappointed. Close to, she saw that they all were coated with a fine layer of dust, a shroud of grey gossamer which lodged in every minute crease, tuck and fold of their petals making them dry like tissue paper. Faded paper flowers. She remembered how, as a small child, she'd made some brightly coloured red and yellow paper flowers at school, had proudly bought them home and stood them on the window ledge in a jam jar of water to grow in the sun; how she had cried and then become angry as the paper faded and crinkled, and how eventually, when her mother had threatened to put them in the bin because they collected dust, she had torn them up herself, ripping the paper off the wire stems and enjoying the destruction of all her painstaking efforts.

She didn't approve of indulging in reminiscence. Savagely she plucked one of the red tulips, the stem breaking easily and cleanly. A drop of sap, milky like semen, oozed onto her finger. A voice behind her made her jump.

'A lovely flower for a lovely lady, eh?'

The bantering tone failed to conceal the derision. Matthews was a senior officer, a burly florid-faced man who chewed gum continually and wore his cap to the back of his head in affectation of an American policeman. Their paths had crossed before, not always amicably, and she was immediately on her guard. Yet now she was at a disadvantage, struggling up from her squatting position, the flower hanging limply from one hand.

'I was just...'

'Nicking Her Majesty's property – carries a heavy sentence, that. Mind you, you can be locked up with me any time,' he drawled, grinning at her embarrassment.

With an effort she gave a twist of a smile, aware that he had forced her into the situation of not being able either to challenge the offensive sexual innuendo without appearing pompous, or to return the mood of the remark without appearing to encourage him.

'How about a coffee in the officers' canteen? It looks like rain and you won't be working here today.' He gave a slight ironic emphasis to the word 'working'.

'Why not?'

Matthews scratched his large belly, sliding one finger in-between the buttons of his shirt and rubbing it back and forth. She imagined his dark body hair rubbing against her smooth skin and felt a sudden and unexpected thrust of revulsion and desire.

'You really don't know?'

'No,' she snapped, impatient at his obvious pleasure in being in possession of information she wasn't. 'But I'm sure you're going to tell me.'

He appeared oblivious to the sarcasm, waiting for her to fully straighten up before speaking in a voice that was heavy with self-importance.

'Lot of trouble inside here last night. Been brewing for some time, we knew that, so it's not as if we was unprepared. Some of the cons got just a little upset because visiting hours had been cut back. Started off with a sit-down when association time was over, then a few chairs got thrown and then the whole bloody balloon went up. Barricades. Demands. The usual few hard cases stirring up the rest of them. One wing more or less put out of action. Didn't you see it on the news this morning?'

She shook her head. She'd spent the morning writing, revising an important chapter, locked in a world of her own creation. Matthews was savouring his moment of triumph. He spoke slowly and deliberately.

'Trouble is, some of 'em in here seem to think they're in a holiday camp rather than a nick. Anyway, it gave us the opportunity to sort out the real troublemakers. You might say we made 'em see things our way.' He jangled the heavy loop of keys that hung from his belt and laughed. 'In fact, if I remember rightly one of 'em was your protegé, Connors isn't it?' His face darkened. 'He was a right little bastard. Did a lot of damage before we got him cornered in his pad. He had a knife, tried to carve up one of our lads before he was overpowered. Pity the knife slipped in the struggle 'cos it didn't half cause a mess. Blood, papers, books all over the shop. They had to hose down the floor afterwards and ditch all his gear. 'Course, he's in the hospital wing now, but once he's able to walk we'll have him shipped out. You're on a loser offering education to scum like that.'

Again the slight stress on the word 'education', as if it was something not quite legitimate, like astrology or ESP, that was believed only by a gullible few. He was watching her closely.

61

She struggled to realign her sense of reality before reaching back, as she often did, for a foothold on conventional responses.

'God, how dreadful... I had no idea... I never thought that... anyway, thanks for... for telling me. I suppose I might as well be off then. I presume there's no classes running today?'

Matthews smirked and shook his head slowly as if communicating with a child. She avoided his gloating eyes, large and pink-rimmed like a pig's.

'Would you tell them at the gate that I've gone?'

'Sure will, pretty lady.'

She felt a pure white flame of hatred towards the coarse, ignorant man leap inside her, but immediately quenched it with a shower of vapid words. 'I was just looking at the flowers. I've always admired them. Such lovely colours. Aren't they wonderful, the way they're always out.'

Her fingers closed around the one she held and crushed it.

Matthews laughed again. 'Well, they would, wouldn't they, being under them all the time.' He pointed upwards, and following the direction of his finger she saw the spotlights punctuating the outside wall at regular intervals, like inverted hooks. 'Artificial light, see? They get it all the night through. Not one square inch of the outside here is left in dark. That's why they do so well. In fact, you could say it's a riot of colour. Yeah, a real riot of colour.' Matthews grinned and chewed on his gum, furiously waiting for an acknowledgement of his wit.

Silently she picked up her bag and turned her back on him and the prison. Then she walked quickly away, head down against the wind, one hand holding her coat closed at the neck. The sky was heavy and slanting spikes of rain were beginning to jab the ground and blacken it. Glancing quickly to either side, she crossed over the road, dropping the flower as she did so. It had stained her palm red. A few seconds later it disappeared under pounding wheels in a spray of dirt and grit.

# Outing

The staff at Sigglesthorpe Sixth Form College bore little relation to their photos, which were taken by Mrs Bream during the staff training week before the start of the Autumn term and then displayed prominently in a glass case in the foyer. For example, Dave Sangster, normally clean shaven, had become so hirsute during the long vacation spent *en famille* in France that some wag labelled his photo 'Yeti'. However, by the end of September with the arrival of the Visa bill (occasioning a not-inconsiderable row over some items purchased in the Duty-Free shop on the return ferry) and his wife Irene's all-month-round PMT, the hair was literally and symbolically shorn. Combined with the strained look induced by the realisation that he had not yet prepared for the new NVQ in *Getting the Most Out of Unemployment*, Dave was all but unrecognisable. Similarly Miss Prendle, Head of Business Studies, refused to have her photo taken and submitted an airbrushed one of her own, which caused much disappointment on the part of male students searching fruitlessly for a sultry blonde and finding instead a stout figure, legs roped with varicose veins and hair several shades darker than the photo suggested, although admittedly with a not unattractive face were it not for the pebble bottomed glasses and tufted moles.

It has to be said that Mrs Bream's camera techniques did not help matters. Her method involved grabbing her subjects, ignoring their pleas to be allowed to comb their hair or remove the crisps from their front teeth, and flattening them against the wall of the staff lounge. The dazed, crazed looks this produced had managed to deter more than a few parents from sending their precious offspring to Sigglesthorpe, concluding as they did that the staff looked as if a psychiatric hospital would be a more appropriate place of work for them. Mrs Bream's chronic alcoholism did not help the developing and printing process either. One year the same member of staff, Mr Whiting – the vice principal after whom Mrs Bream lusted – appeared five times in the glass case, while others made no appearance at all. Adding to this was the mislabelling of the staff's teaching subjects, so it was little wonder that by the end of their first week most new Sigglesthorpe students were confused about their own names, let alone their tutors'.

Mr Whiting aspired to the gold-bordered frame in the middle of the glass case, reserved for the principal's non-likeness. This in fact was a costly studio portrait, paid for by staff selling pedestal mats and toilet seat covers embossed with the college crest. The current principal was soon taking early retirement, thus formalising how he spent his time anyway, and Mr Whiting was confident of not only taking over the gold-bordered frame but also his office, which housed the biggest rubber plant of any Principal's office in the Authority, not to mention the secretarial services of the luscious Miss Potts. Accordingly, at Christmas he decided to throw a small *soirée* to which he invited a few chosen colleagues and senior members of the Authority whom it would be desirable to impress. A non-alcoholic punch, some hot mince pies, turkey vol-au-vents and a little civilised conversation could only benefit his career, particularly if Muriel, his wife, confined herself to the kitchen. She had the amazing capacity of only opening her mouth to change feet, which had caused him much embarrassment in the past. However, she was a good housekeeper and cook so he was reluctant to dispense with her services altogether. He would get thirteen-year-old Harriet to play a violin solo – she'd just got Grade 6 Distinction and her vibrato was quite stunning. He set the date for the last day of the Christmas term, December 18th.

Dave Sangster also had plans for an end-of-term function, and his too was to be a select affair. Invites were issued only to those who were chronically embittered and disillusioned with teaching, and whose social aspirations amounted to a deep seated desire to get thoroughly rat-arsed before falling over. Two NQTs who, on their PGCE year, had had the importance of staffroom networking emphasised and the college caretaker, George, who now only had to attend his Anger Management course fortnightly, made up the numbers. Accordingly, Dave booked a minibus for the 18th December and arranged a circuitous route which took in twelve pubs ending up at Ye Olde Cider Lodge renowned for its scrumpy with the power, not to mention taste, of rocket fuel.

How, at about 11pm, the minibus came to deliver its occupants in varying degrees of drunkenness (ranging from the tearfully sodden Mrs Bream to the loudly snoring Dave Sangster) at Mr Whiting's house was the subject of much debate within Sigglesthorpe College for months to come. Some claimed deliberate tampering with the driver's schedule in order to embarrass either Dave Sangster or Mr Whiting by a party or parties unknown; others claimed the notoriously badly-signposted crossroads at the top of Leminton Hill were to blame. The truth was unlikely ever to be known. No one in the bus subsequently remembered anything, and the driver went off sick the next day with a stress-related illness.

However, some incidents passed into College folklore. Mrs Bream's indecent assault on Mr Whiting on the snooker table might have gone undiscovered were it not for her use of Harriet's violin bow, which occasioned a visit to A&E the next morning where it so happened that a Sigglesthorpe student was on work experience. Similarly, the fact that someone (actually George) had urinated into various bowls of pot-pourri placed around the Whitings' house was reported by their cleaning lady, who also 'did' at the college. Other incidents became the subject of an official memo. Miss Prendle had unfortunately lost her glasses at Ye Olde Cider Lodge when she had been standing on a table demonstrating to the two pale-looking NQTs how her imminent operation for varicose veins would be performed. In her excitement, the glasses had slipped down her nose and onto the floor, whereupon Dave Sangster took a step backwards and crushed them. Three and a half pints of Scrumpy had mitigated Miss Prendle's distress at the broken glasses – shouting *Geronimo* she leapt from the table and, clinging to Dave's back like a huge praying mantis, implored him to give her the ride of a lifetime. Unfortunately, even seven pints of Broddington's Very Old Peculiar could not anaesthetise Dave against this horror and, after she was prised off him by the rest of the group, he was forced to lock himself in the Gents until the time came for the minibus to depart and Miss Prendle could be forcibly restrained inside it. On arrival at the Whitings, however, Miss Prendle's attention was diverted by a blur in the driveway she took to be a past suitor but who was in fact the Senior County Advisor. She was up the path and had his trousers down around his ankles before anyone could stop her. Trying to hobble away, her prey tripped and fell into a rose bush, unfortunately the same one into which the two NQTs, who had bolted from the bus as soon as it had stopped, were puking loudly and extensively.

A cry from the front door was heard, and there was Muriel, dressed in nothing but a large plastic apron usually used for barbeques. Unknown to her husband, Muriel had been attending lectures in Women's Studies at the local Adult

Education Centre. With her assertiveness training reinforced by half a bottle of cooking sherry, she had called the Chair of Governors a boring old fart, had done a complete striptease and was now running around the front garden doing quite unspeakable things with a garden gnome, her large white buttocks gleaming and wobbling in the moonlight. Three of Mr Whiting's guests made a dash for it into one of their cars, and managed to back out of the driveway before Muriel flung herself on their car bonnet, causing the driver to reverse into the minibus. The jolt and the sound of splintering glass woke Dave Sangster up from his *Easy Rider* dream in which he was somehow simultaneously straddling a Harley Davison and the luscious Miss Potts. Out he and the driver jumped, and within seconds a brawl developed which made even college staff meetings look civilised.

The arrival of police, complete with riot shields, batons and sniffer dogs effectively put a bit of a damper on the revelry. The house was turned upside down and everyone was strip-searched for drugs. The two NQTs requested that they be permitted to search each other, but this was turned down, although they were allowed to keep holding hands while a senior officer carried out the task. A number of people appeared in court the following Monday morning and were fined for breaches of the peace, disorderly conduct and committing an indecent offence with a garden gnome. Subsequently, Dave Sangster was last seen boarding a Cross-Channel ferry wearing headband and backpack, and Miss Prendle abandoned teaching in favour of prostitution, which was what she'd always really wanted to do but which her Connexions advisor in Year 11 had advised against.

As for the Whitings, despite some intensive counselling at Relate, Muriel decided that really she was a lesbian and she'd never had much enjoyment from sex, even on those occasions when he'd been considerate and not dressed up in too many of her clothes or tied the ropes too tightly. They had as quiet a divorce as could be arranged after *The Sunday Mirror* had been tipped the wink from someone at the brewery, where Mrs Bream now worked. Mr Whiting did not get the principal's job, which was hardly surprising; after all, he had not gone on nearly as many management courses as the grey suited, grey-faced man who, much sooner than anticipated, did take up the appointment. Mr Whiting's role in the management structure was redefined. He was put in charge of sweeping the courtyard and refilling the condom machine in the boys' toilets, as well as seeing that the glass display case in the foyer was filled with the correct staff photographs. He soon took early retirement. The trouble was, so many of the new staff appointed by the principal over the next few months looked the same, what with their grey suits and their grey faces. He'd shuffle through the photos and have great trouble sorting out who was who. Soon after he left, it was decided that the display case was no longer needed, as it encouraged over-familiarity between staff and students. It was taken down off the wall and thrown into the skip by the boiler room. The glass shattered and the original photos curled up, as if protecting themselves from the shower of splinters.

# Brenda's Blessings

Brenda counted. Every morning, on waking to an alarm set at 6.56, she did a hundred sit-ups on her abdominal cradle; twenty-five with feet placed firmly on the floor, twenty-five with feet in the air, and twenty-five with legs slung to the right side then left. Estimated time for completion – twelve and a half minutes. Showering, drying hair, dressing, breakfasting and opening the bowels normally took a further thirty-five minutes, thirty-nine if she had forgotten her 'All Bran' for supper the night before. Time of departure from house was 7.45, ensuring arrival at work between 8.20 and 8.25, dependant on weather and traffic conditions.

Jim, Brenda's husband for the last fourteen years and four-and-a-half months according to her records (and a 'bloody long time' according to him), usually surfaced about eleven. He never really took much notice of the time but did like to be up, if not dressed, before the arrival of the midday post. He was hairy and faintly smelly, forgetting sometimes to take a shower when his attention was caught by some urgent domestic task, such as reorganisation of his fishing magazines.

Brenda arrived home between 5.30 and 6. 5.30 was good because it allowed her a quick twenty-minute yoga and meditation session before having to start organising Jim to organise the evening meal. Not usually having eaten much during the day, she allowed herself eight hundred calories for the latter, while Jim encouraged his not inconsiderable belly to hold as much as possible. The effect on Jim of his overindulgence was simultaneously somnolence and flatulence. It annoyed Brenda that her frenetic squirting of Floral Bouquet air freshener round Jim as he lay prone on the settee not only failed to rouse him but somehow succeeded in eliciting wind emissions of increased volume and pungency.

Brenda and Jim didn't have any children. Jim had a low sperm count ('Isn't that just typical!' Brenda had exclaimed when the results came back from their GP). However, since she only allowed sex on a Friday night for the two weeks following her period, PMT ruling out the other week, it was hardly surprising, claimed Jim, that this low level of sexual activity had failed to produce results. Brenda retorted that he seemed to be forgetting about holidays, to which Jim had replied that doing it on other days of the week apart from Friday didn't count as sexual experimentation in his book, and how about trying different positions? Brenda replied with a shudder that the alternatives, memorably attempted on their tenth wedding anniversary after a bottle of their neighbour, Mrs Garrett's, homemade rhubarb wine had convinced her that she had got off, if not lightly considering Jim's bulk, at least with some measure of dignity intact.

In actual fact, neither of them really minded their lack of progeny as neither felt they would cope with the unpredictable demands of a child. Brenda couldn't contemplate not knowing how much time and input it would want from her; equally, Jim couldn't imagine being forced to give the amorphous blob that was his day some kind of shape.

So... Brenda grumbled to anyone who would listen (not many did) about Jim – about his laziness, his sloppiness, his lack of energy and drive, while Jim complained that Brenda had a compulsive personality disorder.

And then everything changed.

Not at first. After all, Howard was only four-and-a-half inches of furry rodent in a small cage, and it would just be for a fortnight while she was in hospital having her veins done, a tearful Mrs Garrett had pleaded. Brenda was not keen, but even she could see it would be very difficult to refuse. Their elderly neighbour had done them many good turns over the years, if you excluded the unfortunate rhubarb wine incident. Jim could deal with it, she decided, as she pencilled in Hamster Duties – feeding, exercising, grooming and cleaning cage – against his job schedule for the week. She decided that the animal would be best in the garage, and indeed that was where Howard remained for the first three days, until Jim said that it would be more convenient to move the cage into the utility room. Brenda opened her mouth to object and then closed it again. She had to admit that in her daily trip to the garage to put the newspaper on the recycling pile, she had found there was something soothing about watching Howard nibble at his food, drink from his water bottle and scamper round his wheel. Moreover, Jim did seem to be performing his Hamster Duties with uncharacteristic conscientiousness, and as yet there was no trace of the animal smell she had so dreaded.

After a week Howard's cage had become a fixture on one of the kitchen work surfaces. They had both worried that the utility room wasn't warm enough and, as Brenda said, it would kill Mrs Garrett if anything happened to Howard. In fact what killed Mrs Garrett was a nasty case of food poisoning following her successful operation. The local NHS hospital led the world in pioneering new laser techniques for treating varicose veins, but had failed to master elementary rules of food hygiene. There were only three mourners at her funeral the following week – Brenda, Jim and a shifty looking nephew who displayed an unseemly impatience to get back to the house afterwards and make an inventory of its contents. Brenda and Jim decided not to mention Howard.

'I'm sure he's pining,' Jim said, on the evening of the funeral, and Brenda had to agree that Howard did appear listless, his fur not so glossy and healthy-looking as usual. They tried chopping up sticks of celery and carrot and poking them through the bars of the cage, but Howard just gave them a soulful look and retreated into a corner.

A few days later it was obvious that something was seriously wrong. Brenda had come down as usual at 7.25 to have her mug of herbal tea, half a grapefruit (segmented the night before) and two Ryvitas spread thinly with honey. She was shocked to find Howard huddled in a corner of his cage, shaking as if he was having some kind of fit. On closer inspection, she saw that his eyes were dull and that patches of his fur were greyish. In a panic, she woke Jim who was up, dressed and downstairs faster than she would have thought possible. His verdict was that an immediate visit to the vet's was called for.

Brenda was thrown into panic. Not only did she not know which vet to use, what their opening times were or how you made an appointment, but it would mean she would be late for work, given that the car would be needed to transport Howard. She stood rooted to the spot while Jim, having uttered a few reassuring grunts, went off to consult the Yellow Pages. Brenda felt beads of sweat prickle her forehead as she looked at the hands of the clock moving inexorably round, eating up the time. Already it was 7.52 and, even if she jumped in the car and abandoned Jim and Howard, she would still be late. But she couldn't abandon them: Howard's life could be at stake! She was responsible. As soon as Jim had finished on the phone she would phone the office, but what time could she tell them? If she went in after lunch she'd have the morning appointments to reschedule, which would throw her whole week out. Perhaps she could say she was sick, she knew that's what lots of them did, but then she'd have to decide what her fictional illness was and how long it was going to last.

7.56. Her hands were shaking. A sob escaped from her throat, a gurgly choked sound followed by another. Suddenly it was all too much – the job, the travelling, the burden of having Jim to organise, Mrs Garrett's death, the memory of the two of them at the windswept crematorium watching the cheap coffin disappearing into the furnace, memories of other coffins. A blurred image, one she'd successfully filed away with many others from long ago, came suddenly and sharply into focus. A small child huddled in the corner of her bedroom frantically counting: a hundred and the worst of the screams would be over, two hundred and fifty and there would be the slam of the door, five hundred and then it would be safe.

Brenda moved towards Howard's cage, opened its door and extended her arm inside. Gingerly, she reached for the creature. She had never touched him before. Jim had. In the evening, she'd surreptitiously watched him as she pretended to read her daily allocation of fifty pages from a Booker-shortlisted novel; watched as his large red hands cradled the small animal and he'd stroked the back of its head with his forefinger. Now Howard was in her cupped hands and she could feel the frantic pulsing of his heart against her palm. His whiskers tickled the backs of her fingers, his claws scratched feebly at her skin. She brought him up to her face and smelt. Straw, fur, dampness, life. She tightened her hold. If she squeezed tightly enough she could splinter his little bones, crush his internal organs. But why do that? Desperately she sought to fight her way out of the present by repeating her mantra: house / job / husband / security / holidays / a system that works. House job husband security holidays a system that works. Housejobhusbandsecurity holidaysasystemthatworks. Counting her blessings.

She didn't hear Jim come back into the kitchen. She wasn't aware of him watching her, first with amazement then with compassion as she held Howard to her chest, as if in supplication, unaware of the greeny-black smears he was depositing on her fresh white shirt (white with the navy-blue trouser suit Mondays and Tuesdays, pale blue with the grey on Wednesdays and a skirt and jumper for the rest of the week. Saturdays, jeans and a sweatshirt, a dress if going out in the evening, Sundays similar). She gently rocked him back and forth.

'Brenda?' Jim said softly.

She turned to face him and her expression was empty. 'I don't know what I should be doing, Jim.'

'It's okay. Let's get going. I've got the engine running. Put him back into the cage and then I'll put it on the back seat.'

Brenda couldn't remember how long the journey took, or how long they had to wait for Howard to be seen; how long it was before he recovered, she recovered, or when it was that she handed over control to Jim. Well, not complete control obviously. She might have had a bit of a funny turn, but there had to be limits with someone like Jim whose idea of a social life consisted of putting two pairs of waders into the back of the car.

Brenda had almost stopped counting now. She felt heavy and lethargic, spending many evenings in her chair by the French windows looking out over the garden, once a neatly manicured lawn with regimented flowerbeds but now a tousled, fragrant tangle, the lines between beds and lawn impossible to distinguish. She looked over at Jim who was finishing off a list.

'Just four months, two weeks and five days left, according to my calculations,' he said proudly.

Brenda smiled, pulling up her T-shirt to feel her belly. A line of hairs arrowed thickly down from her navel and she ran her hand over them. She was growing fur and she liked it.

# Listening

At the moment of impact, a dull thud, the crying stopped.

Huddled in her woolly sleep-suit she looked like a small animal that had been knocked down on the road. There was a marvellous sense of softening when the noise ceased, as if the air itself relaxed and hung loose around me. I sank down into the wicker nursing chair, closed my eyes and absorbed the peace into every pore of my skin as a dry sponge does water; took deep shuddering breaths while the silence swelled me, fleshed me, bulged my veins and my old self budded beneath my skin to be released. I don't know what time it was, maybe three or four in the morning, but I was aware of every breath, every tick, every rustle in the universe. Far, far away a clock chimed the hour – I could hear people turning in their beds, cats stalking the back ways, clouds scudding across the night sky.

The darkness pressing against my lids was a blank piece of film through which the familiar images of my surroundings slowly began to seep and imprint themselves. First the small room, once study now nursery: white crib draped with lace, soft piles of blankets and towels, lemon and white ruched curtains, a cream carpet. Then, in sudden sharp focus, a mobile of clowns, heads drooping, suspended from a plastic scaffold over the crib; a puppet hanging on the wall with limbs spread-eagled as if on a rack, its face the chalky whiteness of death. Enter a woman, thin with hollow smudged eyes, rocking her baby backwards and forwards with an increasingly desperate ferocity until it leaves her arms, moves through space and drops onto the floor.

I screwed my eyes up tightly so the picture dissolved in an explosion of yellow glittering stars. Rewound. Relaxed the eyes. Replayed and replayed until the edges of the images bent, furred, became fluid and finally swam away. I dozed. When I finally opened my eyes the sense of liquescence momentarily returned. The room was dappled with shadows thrown by the night-light. Then the pink bundle lying at my feet shifted and sighed. The knowledge that she was alive must surely have been accompanied by overwhelming, sickening relief, but that I can't remember.

Pearl had cried since birth. Obviously there were times when she didn't – when she slept, ate, was bathed, played – logically I know now that must be so, but at the time the only truth I recognised was that inward one which told me she cried incessantly. Sometimes it was a furious red-throated howl, more often it was a low persistent mewling or a long drawn-out moan to herself, which quickly sparked into a series of staccato demands for attention. None of the suggested remedies had any effect. She went on crying. Day and night, night and day she cried. I felt sure that sooner or later she would have to stop, that it was impossible for her miniature sound-producing equipment to endure much longer. It was as if my ears suffered continual interference when they tried to tune into any other sounds. They ached with the effort of carrying on a phone conversation while staying on constant alert. I would lie in bed, tensed, waiting for the grizzling to amplify into a proper cry. If I did get to sleep I'd imagine her noise and jolt awake. The revving of a car outside the flat would make me freeze in mid-action; out shopping the sound of any child would cause my finely-tuned nerves to quiver with anxiety. I felt as if each hair on my skin was a fine delicate antenna for picking up her call. I loathed the apparent transformation that had taken place – from a woman in her mid-thirties, confident in job and relationships, to this pathetic sexless being who looked back at me, grey-faced, from the mirror each morning with no other aim beyond that of making it through another day. There were people – health visitor, midwife, my G.P. – who flitted behind me in the mirror mouthing suggestions, but they were only shadows. My friend Elsa repeatedly invited me down to the Community Centre.

'C'mon Jools, there's an open meeting tonight after the talk and we've organised some booze for later on. You know you'd enjoy it.'

'No, I don't think so.'

'Is it the baby you're worried about? I didn't mean leave her behind. Bring her along. There's plenty of pairs of hands just waiting for a chance to cuddle her.'

(Hands more capable than mine.)

'I don't really feel like it, Else. Honestly. It's such a faff to get her ready and she might need feeding.'

'So you feed her there. No problem.'

(Not to her. Nothing was.)

'I can't...'

'I suppose the proud father is coming round, is that it?'

Imperceptible to anyone who didn't know her like I did, the distaste with which she imbued that reference to John.

'No! Well, yes he might be. I don't know.'

'It's time you remembered who's on your side, kid. Who listened and cared, came with you to the scans, read all the books, rubbed your back. It sure as hell wasn't that man of yours.'

(She's right.)

'I know that and I'm grateful, Else. But it's different now. I can't explain it. I want to come out but...'

'But...?'

'It's like it's just her and me and the more difficult she is and the more she needs me the more I have to stay.'

'By 'her' I take it you mean the baby?'

'By 'the baby' I take it you mean Pearl?'

Once I would have taken up the challenge of this opening spat for a full-length exchange of verbal punches. Now I meekly put myself on the ropes; I shrugged, lowered my eyes and nibbled my already badly-chewed nails. Elsie was a natural bare-fisted fighter. In everything she did, she battled – for causes, her friends, herself. It was self-perpetuating – the fighting kindling her energy. She could accept my relationship with John and the other ones before him, could accept my wanting to have a baby. What she couldn't comprehend was this ready surrender. She raised one of her finely-arched eyebrows (surely she didn't pluck them, I suddenly thought, completely irrelevantly), and as she turned her head in preparation for leaving, her long earrings of jet and silver tapped against the side of her slender neck. With her closely-cropped cap of silky hair and boyish body she resembled a wild, graceful bird, and in a rush I remembered why I loved her. I smiled and it seemed to take her as much by surprise as it did me.

'Look, Jools, I'm no good at this kind of thing. Give me a ring when you feel ready okay? And if you want any help...' She was at the door, rattling the handle, furious at her own uncustomary awkwardness. 'Oh shit, why did you have to go and fuck everything up?'

John did visit fairly regularly at first. I couldn't really understand why, unless it was out of a mistaken sense of loyalty. He didn't know what to do with Pearl any more than I did, and I used to see how many times I could intercept his surreptitious glances at the clock. After half an hour:

'How's she feeding now?'

'Okay.'

'Still three-hourly?'

'More or less.'

'I bought you a bottle of Guinness. Meant to be good when you're breast feeding. Oh yes, and this is for her Ladyship.' He held up a teddy, complete with garish Mexican hat and poncho, and squeezed its bulbous tummy to produce a squeak.

'Shh... you might wake her. Thanks a lot.'

'Is it okay?'

'What?'

'The beer, the toy. God, I don't know, everything.'

'Yeah, it's all okay. Don't worry.' His eighth covert glance at the clock. About time to let him off the hook now. 'Isn't it time you were going?'

He tried not to show relief as he got up, looked at his watch and feigned surprise at the time. I realised what an unconvincing actor he was – indeed for him there was no difference between his professional and personal posturing – and wondered why I'd refused to acknowledge it before. 'Christ! I'd no idea it was so late. I must fly or I'll be late for rehearsal. Look, I'll pop in the day after tomorrow. Sure there's nothing you want?'

'No, nothing. Bye John.'

'Bye.' His lips brushed my cheek, and while it seemed incredible that there had ever been any kind of connection between the two of us now, ironically, the indissoluble connection started to cry in the next room.

And of course there was my mother. There always had been.

'What are you going to do, darling?'

'Have a bath, then try to get past the front page of *The Guardian*. If Pearl doesn't wake.'

'Are you trying to be facetious, Julia? No, I'm sorry, that's unfair of me. You're still in a very delicate state. What of course I meant was what are your plans for the future? How does John fit into all this? Has marriage been discussed? What surname are you going to give little Pearl?'

'Oh Mum, for God's sake...'

'It's no good adopting that attitude, Julia. These questions are not going to simply disappear. I quite accept that the modern way of doing things is very different to how your father and I were brought up, but the fact remains that we would like to know how things stand.'

'I don't know how things stand, Mum. I'm here and I've got Pearl, isn't that enough for the moment? It's just about all I can cope with.'

'Well, I can't say that all this is any different from how you've treated your father and I in the past. Always kept us in the dark about your plans until everything was a *fait accompli*. It was just the same when you turned down your university offer and took the job on the magazine instead. We didn't know a thing about it until the day before you started. It made us look so silly.'

'As soon as I make any decisions, you and Dad will be the first to know. Or perhaps you'd rather make them yourself and save me the bother of having to tell you?'

'That was really most unkind, Julia, and most unwarranted. We only want to help.'

As she fumbled in her handbag for a hanky, from the bedroom came the unmistakeable sounds of Pearl stirring. I stiffened.

'Please, Mum, will you go now.'

'Well, if that's all the thanks I get after...'

'Go! Just go!' I begged. Somehow I felt as though the steadily increasing volume of crying could break down, dismantle brick by brick, the wall my mother and I had erected between ourselves over the years. I feared its removal. She, of course, recognised only rejection.

None of them would listen to any voice except their own.

None of them could seem to understand that it was our own private hell, mine and Pearl's, and we would survive – or not – together.

As days then weeks passed, I struggled to comfort and soothe the squalling bundle that I held tightly to my chest – that I rocked, swayed, jiggled, stroked. Periodically she would quieten and fix me with her pale blue eyes; her eyelids would start fluttering and close, becoming almost translucent as they did so. The little face would relax, the pouchy cheeks slacken and the moist circle of mouth hang partially open as her breathing became slower and steadier. Gradually I would stop the movement and lay her gently down, extricating my arm as slowly as possible, leaving my body bent in an arc over the crib or pram. At once her face would scrunch up, contort, turn from side to side as if trying to fight away the open space around her; a few deep breaths and then the crying would restart. Straightening up, I would experience the floor beneath my feet tilting slightly as if on board ship, before I stooped to pick her up once more. Sleep, rest, were things that existed in a previous life. I yearned for them, lusted for them as I had once done for others' bodies, but they eluded me, skipping and dancing just beyond reach. The months of tiredness began to desiccate my body. My eyes hurt, back ached, scalp itched. My skin became dry and flaky, my lips blistered and my tongue was cracked leather.

* * *

It had poured down the night she was born. From my bed I watched the rain sluice down the windows and the car headlights give watery blinks as they crawled up the drive. Wired up to a foetal monitoring machine, its rhythmic bleep and swoosh made me feel that I was experiencing the same prenatal state as my unborn child. The white walls of the hospital room seemed to curve around me like a giant egg as I lay cocooned in this spherical cell, swaddled by the warmth, the dimmed light and soothed by the pulse of my electronic leech. Despite the taut hump of belly looming in front of me and the pains coming with increasing frequency – like iron bands being tightened across my middle – I was unafraid and even obtained a perverse kind of pleasure from them. My pains were the black side of orgasm. As I successfully mounted and rode each one I was suffused, as it receded, with a feeling of fullness and wellbeing. I remember looking at the huge clock opposite and watching the dark black strokes of the minutes being eaten up by the big hand and feeling a real achievement when two o'clock was reached. I've judged everything that's happened in my life as before or after that point.

Afterwards the pain entered another dimension. The baby started to exert her will for independent existence and at the same time as recognising it, I hated it. My first parental act. Her first filial act. I wanted her to stay there inside me, parasitic, silent, bathed in the warm wash of amniotic fluid. As the night went on, sweat trickled down under my arms, down my back and into the creases of my groin. It ran down my forehead and into my eyes. Still I did not begrudge the pain. But with the breaking of my waters it ceased being a localised sensation and pounded and twisted my whole body. Contractions took place in my hands, my forehead, my toes and my neck. I felt as though the core of my body was being turned this way and that on a fruit squeezer until the last drop of juice was extracted. I heard my own voice, as if from a distance, cry and shout and I felt the prick of a needle in my thigh.

Pearl fought for her freedom. She scratched and kicked to be released and I spread my legs as far as they could possibly go, like a log that has been cleaved into a giant V by an axe. Yet even then, not far enough, and I sensed rather than actually felt the snip of skin as the midwife cut into the soft folds of tissue to widen me. Then all that was left was a push and a strain as I simultaneously emptied bowels and uterus. She burrowed her way out of my flesh and shot out in a slimy pellet like a skinned rabbit. As the midwife clamped then cut the cord, she started a muffled crying; when she put her to my breast she at first sucked greedily, then turned her head away and cried in disgust. A few minutes later I remember looking down and seeing in a dish on the trolley the placenta, a grotesque slab of bluish-red liver which I hadn't even been aware of passing. I was shocked at what my body had spontaneously aborted and somehow it didn't seem right that I should lose a part of myself so casually, so unceremoniously. I found myself trying to remember my soul-searching of seven months previously when I had listened to Elsa and others try and persuade me to have the contents of my womb similarly disposed of. Now that vital part of me which had succoured and nourished my daughter lay useless at my side ready, presumably, to be tipped into a hospital incinerator that gobbled foetuses and placentas with equal relish. Didn't animals eat their afterbirths because they were so full of vitamins and goodness? And witches too? Suddenly I retched violently and there was a flurry of activity around my bed. It was that night for the first time that I had a vivid dream, induced no doubt by all the pethidine, that was to continue to haunt me for the next six months.

Look.

I am the chief guest at a banquet – all the other guests are already seated and I am conducted to the top of the table by a footman carrying a candelabra. The room is large but lit only by candles so the faces of those present are unclear, almost molten, in the yellowy luminescence. Occasionally, guttering flames catch some item of jewellery at a pale wrist or throat and it flashes insolently. The air, warm and sweet, is filled with the heady scent from bowls of flowers positioned the length of the table. I sit at its head and look down upon a sea of white damask on which float armadas of silver dishes, platters, cutlery and cruet. A silver salver, grander than any of those on the table and borne aloft by another footman, is placed in front of me. The gentle buzz of conversation ceases and expectation hangs in the air as heavily as the perfume of the flowers. The salver is covered with a vast bell-shaped lid, but even so the juices and aromas which creep from under it make all those present lick their lips and sniff the air with anticipation. They crane their heads forward to look. I stand and with a flourish try to remove the lid. It sticks. Again I pull at it and again. Beads of perspiration stand out on my forehead and my hands grow clammy with the effort, until eventually, with a deep groan, I yank the lid off. There in the middle of the salver huddles the placenta. It has gone completely blue, is shrivelled, dry and foul smelling. The stench seems to make its way down the table and, like dominoes falling, people draw back their heads in revulsion. It's then that I notice that the cloth is not pure white but spotted with bloodstains just like the hospital gown that I'm wearing; that the cutlery is in fact surgical instruments and that the flowers, pink veined and tumescent, are floating and drinking from bowls of bright red blood.

As I gaze in horror I recognise some of the guests too; there, halfway down on the right is my mother – she is writing lists onto the tablecloth, shaking her head from time to time as if there is something she cannot quite get right. Almost opposite her Elsa, beautiful and deadly as a black swan, is looking angry as she repeatedly jabs a scalpel into a soft peach. Then John, further down on the same side as my mother, his face expressing the same awkwardness, irritation and embarrassment as it did when I first told him I was pregnant.

There are others too – my gynaecologist, landlord, work colleagues. As the stench becomes more and more overpowering, I see that the dish no longer holds the placenta but a pile of my own shit – satiny, gently steaming, getting bigger by the minute. As my face burns I hear the cries of a hungry baby and I begin frantically searching for it, running down the length of the table, grabbing at people, looking in dishes, knocking one of the bowls over and causing a huge heart shaped stain, a badge of my shame, to spread over the cloth. As the cries get louder my searching becomes more intense, much to everyone's amusement. Some of the tapes are missing at the back of my gown and I put one hand behind my back in a desperate attempt to keep it together. All the guests are out of their places now, milling around, and I see John grab Elsa, lie her back onto the table, pull up her long black dress until it covers her face and fuck her, throwing back his head, his face white and contorted in a deathlike grimace. Then he pulls her up and they both take a deep bow, but no one except me appears to notice; they laugh and drink, a few start to dance to the string quartet which has appeared at the far end of the room, making my attempts to locate the source of the crying even harder. I want to scream myself, but when I open my mouth no sound comes out. Then I realise the baby's crying is from within me, it is my own unuttered screams, and I struggle to rip the front of my body open so as to tear it out.

I awoke to find myself tearing at the front of my nightie, and Pearl tended to by a midwife at the other side of the room.

'My, you're a deep sleeper to be sure. This little darling's being yelling her head off for the last ten minutes.'

'Sorry.' The absence of any accusatory tone in her voice only exacerbated my sense of guilt. I felt hollow and ran my hand down over the unaccustomed flatness of my belly.

'Shall I take her now?'

She deftly swaddled Pearl and bought her over to me. I disengaged one pendulous breast, a huge blue-veined gourd, and she fixed on to it immediately. The midwife drew back one of the curtains and lent her elbows on the windowsill.

'Looks like the rain has stopped, pet. That's good. At least it means I won't be getting soaked going home. And isn't that a rainbow I can see over there?'

Maybe I was at the wrong angle but I couldn't see it. A large fat tear rolled down my cheek and I put out my tongue to catch it, just like we used to do with rain when we were kids.

* * *

This time, I let the runnels of tears stream uncaught down my face. They splashed onto my chest and made my nightie so damp it stuck to my skin. But somehow they vitalised me. I got up from the chair and lay down beside Pearl on the floor. I couldn't see her face, just her perfectly-shaped bullet of a head, the fringe of pale hair lying over the collar of the pink suit. I stroked her head.

(They, whoever 'they' are, say babies are defenceless. It's one of the many lies you are told. As well as the crying with which she battered me, Pearl had an armoury of defences – she could dig, scratch, grip, pummel. It was me who was left defenceless.)

I felt for the warmth of her neck and encircled my fingers round it. A pulse fluttered against my fingertips.

(I thought I was well protected, I honestly did. I had patience, enough money, a healthy body and mind and, above all, the desire to nurture and raise my baby – a desire which had embedded itself as inexplicably yet as firmly as the fertilised egg. And yet my baby had succeeded in breaking through the lot, exposing my glossy veneer of self-knowledge to be nothing better than dry, crumbly plaster which flaked off as easily as my skin.)

I squeezed the hand that was round her neck oh-so-very gently.

(It wasn't that I snapped – that implies a sudden breaking, a clean crisp action. That night I dropped Pearl was the final inevitable movement of the past six months, the peak of the curve on which I'd risen and now, as I lay beside her in the cold early morning light, on which I rode back down to the oneness within myself, the completion, that I'd surrendered at her birth.)

I ran my hand down the tiny knobbles of her vertebrae – felt her well-bolstered little bottom, the fatty thighs, the ridges of her perfect toes. So substantial she was and yet at the same time so breakable: bones that could be bent like rubber, tiny lungs stoppered with a pillow, neck wrung like a kitten's, perfectly-proportioned skull shattered like a baby bird's.

She gave a deep sigh, turned her head on one side and, eyes still closed, threw one arm out. Then, for the first time, I saw her as more than an extension of myself. I saw John in her. Not in her nose or mouth or shape of her head – nothing as specific as that – although maybe it was something to do with her warm breath and the gesture of the arm flung out which gave me a momentary flashback to Sunday mornings and skin and hair entwining in a tangle of sheets and love. No, much more importantly I saw her ownness, her separateness too. It was then that I could let go, then that I could finally stop fighting and accept the inevitable. For the next three hours we lay there together, fast asleep.

In due course I rang for an ambulance, and back we were both taken to the same hospital. Trundling trolley, squeaky shoes on polished floors, white coats, cold hard metal placed on warm freshly woken flesh, large gentle hands cupping Pearl's head as they had done at the moment of birth all those centuries ago, manipulation of limbs, searching looks and questions. Examinations, X-Rays, scribbled notes. Sitting in

Sister's office talking to a weary young doctor who could almost have been my son, his youthful unblemished face furrowed with the effort to understand what I was saying. I admitted I'd dropped her. That I'd been careless. That I was tired. Somebody from Social Services was summoned and duly arrived, looking harassed. More interviews, more note-taking amid the clatter of early-morning hospital routine. Eventually it was decided I could take Pearl home, after she had stayed in for the rest of that day for observation. She was alright: she had mild concussion but they reckoned there wouldn't be any long-term damage. She'd have to come back for periodical checkups and a social worker would call regularly. I would not be prosecuted. There was a possibility that she would be put on the 'At Risk' register; nobody wanted to listen when I said that she wasn't at risk anymore. She was quiet from then on, you see. She might cry a bit when hungry, but once I picked her up it would stop at once and she'd gaze up at me with those clear blue eyes, as blue as drunken cornflowers, and perhaps I only imagined the flicker of fear that passed across them.

It was me who was at risk, on those rare occasions when my time was unoccupied by job, friends or a man. At home, at night, just the two of us – it was then that the silence would engulf me, threaten to drown me in the same way as once the crying had. My sleep was silent too – no more dreams of banquets redolent with images ripe for psychoanalysis. No more dreams of anything. Sometimes I would wake in the night to find I had been rubbing myself, and my small cry of pleasure/pain – I could not distinguish which – would be eaten up by the darkness. The silence, my life without dreams, was my punishment for acting out of love. Self-love, I know, and that's what we mothers are not permitted to have. A woman's right to choose only exists for that mere pinprick of time; every night after that, the cell door is locked, the double doors on the prison landings are bolted, the iron gates of the mental hospitals clang shut, and the swing doors leading from the mother and baby unit are firmly fastened. All over the land, front doors are sealed, and we are left alone with ourselves, our babies and our inadequacies.

But if that sounds like I'm attempting self-justification, I'm not. Really. I know that I defended my self, my sanity, at the cost of my beautiful daughter's well-being. It was and is unforgivable.

God knows I die a little every time I remember it.

Listen.

I can hear nothing.

# Staying Afloat

I met my psychiatrist again in the pool. I say 'met', actually we collided as I was halfway through my twenty-fourth length. He was executing a rather enthusiastic butterfly action, while I ploughed steadily up and down doing breast stroke. As he bought his wheeling arms downwards he clipped me on the neck. Knocked sideways, I went under, and for the brief moment before surfacing I found myself back again in that strange disconnected world of contorted faces and threshing limbs. Yet once my head was above water, I was furious because of course my hair was ruined and there are limits to even waterproof mascara; I knew I would have panda-like smudges around my eyes and that the remaining change from my housekeeping would have to be fed into the hairdryer.

I steeled myself to stop him and say something when we passed on my twenty-sixth length. I knew this might prove difficult as most of the people there were serious swimmers, and resented being forced to make any deviation from their chosen course. The men tended to hog the pool – steaming backwards and forwards, puffing and hissing like leaky engines, running down anyone who dared to stray onto their track of water. Most of them wore goggles, and the addition by some of flesh-coloured bathing caps suggested a grotesque swarm of alien water-insects; whereas the women, holding their heads stiffly and awkwardly out of the water like proud horses on invisible reins, tended to be nervously looking round to ensure they could take evasive action if need be and consequently steered a slightly more wavery furrow.

Anyway, I had made up my mind to complain or, if not, at least to show by my expression what I felt. As I turned at the end I decided on side-stroke so as to make the confrontation easier. However by then he was doing backstroke, his feet churning up a white spume, arms cleaving anti-clockwise like an overwound toy, and therefore it was only as we drew parallel that I recognised him. It was the nose that did it. Shiny red, as if it alone, detached from the rest of his face, had been left out in the sun too long, it was aquiline with thin pinched nostrils from which sprouted tufts of grey hair. Having looked up at it countless times from my supine position on the couch, it identified him beyond doubt. That and his size – he was a huge man, well over six foot with broad shoulders supporting a squarish head. When I realised it was him, I didn't remonstrate about the collision but spent my twenty-seventh, eighth and ninth lengths wondering whether it would be the done thing to reintroduce myself. By the time I'd reached my Wednesday target of thirty he'd got out, and while I dried myself, rubbing oil into heels and elbows, moisturising the rest of my body, I racked my brains for his name. So much of that time was still hazy. Binton, Brenton. Branton, something like that. He'd been considered one of the top men in the field, so I'd been told, although presumably he had retired since then. Certainly, he'd got me straightened out, and under his supervision my days had reassumed order. In the morning I'd take little mauve tablets like the Parma violet sweeties we used to eat as children; then, if I felt bad at any point in the day there were capsules – Red Devils he'd called them – and lovely flat tablets, precious discs of compressed white powder, that ensured oblivion at night-time. And we talked. About my childhood, my relationship with my father, the pressure of coping with three little ones and Harry away a lot of the time. My difficulty in coming to terms with my roles as mother and wife.

Dressed, I emerged from the cubicle, and while I did my hair examined my figure in the long mirror. Really not bad for thirty-eight, though only constant exercise and rigorous diet kept it under control. With a shudder I thought back to after Roddy's birth, when my weight had soared to a shameful thirteen stone. I'd simply let myself go, so Dr. Brenton/ Branton/Brinton had told me. Looking at my watch, I realised that it was nearly 3:15 and that if I didn't hurry I wouldn't make the school gates in time. I hurried out of the changing rooms, and as I pushed my way through the chrome turnstiles in the foyer, out of the corner of my eye I could have sworn I saw Dr. B. fastening on roller skates! That did seem rather unlikely, and I pushed the unsettling impression away as firmly as I did the water when swimming.

After that he was there every Monday and Wednesday, always in the pool before I was and out before I'd finished. We'd taken to acknowledging each other's presence by a curt nod or smile, but from the glazed look in his eyes I could tell he didn't remember me. Not surprising really. I knew he specialised in cases of post-natal depression and he must have treated thousands like me in the intervening five years.

The first time he did it I couldn't believe what had happened. I was at the deep end, holding onto the side, treading water while I took a breather. I'd done thirty-four lengths and was feeling pretty proud of myself. Swimming toned up more muscles than any other sport, so I'd been told, and while I waited I pinched a layer of flesh on my thigh to try and break done some of the fatty tissue. Dr. B. swam up next to me, touched the side, took a deep breath and flipped over underwater to turn. As he did so, he hooked his thumbs under the back of his swimming trunks and quickly rolled them down then up again. I had a momentary glimpse of his moon-like buttocks glistening white and smiling up at me from under the greenish-blue water and then he was gone.

Obviously no-one else had noticed, not that the pool was very crowded anyway. The few bodies there were continued to automatically make their way backwards and forwards, forwards and backwards.

It made me think I must have forgotten my tablet at lunchtime, or perhaps taken two by mistake, but it happened again a week later and once more after a break of three weeks. I unsuccessfully tried persuading myself it was accidental. I wondered whether it was only me he did it to. I even contemplated going to the city's other pool; but it was a longish bus ride away, as Harry insisted on having the car, and I wouldn't have been able to make it back for the children. However, before long his behaviour became so bizarre that it did attract the attention of the other pool users, not to mention the attendants. First of all he started to swim widths rather than lengths, slicing across the lanes of the other swimmers with a frenzied crawl; then he did zig-zags from one end to the other, completely ruining anyone's attempts to keep in a straight line and turning the whole pool into one vast turbulence; it bubbled and slopped as his massive body flailed about. People had their faces splashed, their heads knocked, they swallowed great mouthfuls of heavily-chlorinated water.

It wasn't that I wanted to, but somehow I found I couldn't stop myself from remembering how once there had been no pattern to my thoughts, just a chaotic bumping and jostling of random feelings and sensations. And as Dr. B.'s movements became increasingly erratic, occasioning several warnings from the attendants, so mine became less purposeful, especially on a Friday when Dr. B. wasn't there and when I normally occupied my mind with working out the menus and shopping lists for the weekend. I took to swimming a couple of lengths half-heartedly, then floating on my back in the shallow end contemplating the coloured spheres that hung from the roof of the modern sports centre like oversized golf balls. I thought of coming round after the electric shock therapy, lying on the stretcher and, by blinking rapidly, making the lights above explode into a myriad different colours. And there was the noise – high-pitched shrieks and screams echoing off the tiled walls and being absorbed into my seemingly porous head.

They finally took him away when he stood on the diving board and urinated into the pool. I just happened to be watching as he slipped his thingy from out of his funny old-fashioned swimming trunks – they were navy-blue in that sort of coarse fuzzy material with a white cord around the middle – and casually produced this magnificent arc of golden liquid which rose then fell into the water with a delicate pattering sound. It seemed to go on for ages too; later I wondered if he'd had it all planned and had filled his bladder especially. As people gradually became aware of what was happening they froze and all noise ceased; you could just hear this pitter-patter, like gentle rain splashing into a puddle. For a brief moment, all eyes were on him. There he stood above us on the top board, head thrown back, legs akimbo; a general, a king, while we, his subjects far below, looked up in awe. Then of course all hell broke loose. People started turning away, talking, shaking their heads in disgust; one attendant blew on his whistle while another ran along the poolside and started to climb the steps. Dr. B., having shaken off the last few drops and readjusted himself, turned around and saw his pursuer. With a yell of glee and shouting 'Bombs Away!', he ran to the very end of the board and jumped, hugging his knees so that when he hit the water it caused a minor tidal wave to roll towards the shallow end. He then proceeded to swim round and round in circles, doing doggy paddle, while the two attendants debated how to get him out. Eventually the manager was summoned over the tannoy and along he bustled, a dapper little man wearing blazer, red tie and an air of prim efficiency. Crouching on the pool edge, he attempted to reason with Dr. B. who, having completely ignored him for a good five minutes, then suddenly swam over, reached up, grabbed his ankle and pulled him into the water. Presumably the manager couldn't swim, judging by the fuss he made and the speed with which a lifebelt was thrown to him. It seemed funny to me that a man, especially one like him who was in charge of the place, hadn't learnt to swim. Anyway, eventually burly reinforcements were summoned, and both he and Dr. B. (who was by this time behaving properly by swimming quietly up and down in the now near-empty pool) were hauled out. Dr. B., looking slightly bemused, was led away by the arm into the office.

Completely bonkers, round the bend, an utter loony – so I was told people said.

Dr. B. was put away in a private home somewhere, which wasn't fair really. I mean, everyone pees in the water, that's why it stings your eyes so I'm told; it's just that most people do it discreetly. As for me, I lost my enthusiasm for swimming. I went less and less often, spending the time lying on my bed, or the grass outside if it was fine, reading a book and eating an illicit bar of chocolate. It was what I always used to enjoy doing before the children were born. Of course I'm putting on weight now, as Harry has been quick to point out, but at least I don't seem to need the tablets as much as before. Even being late for picking the children up doesn't get me in a flap like it used to. And I laugh more. Just the thought of that golden parabola of pee and all that followed can sometimes make me laugh until the tears run down my face, streaking my make-up until, so Harry tells me, I look half-crazy.

I tell him I quite like the way I look.

# Finding the Way

Near Glaisdale they leave the car at the ford, slightly skewed because of the uneven ground. Once outside, the rush of wind is dizzying as they struggle to change into walking boots and Anna braces herself against the side of the car.

'Don't you think maybe we should...'

'Don't worry. They always exaggerate these weather reports. The sky doesn't look too bad and we're prepared, remember?' Graham slides the Ordnance Survey map in its plastic wallet out from under his jacket, then carefully tucks it away again, patting his breast pocket as he does so.

'Whistle. Compass. Chocolate.' Each of the words is punctuated with a gesture indicating their whereabouts on his person; he draws out a string from under his polo neck, pats his left hand pocket and then his right.

A cock of his head, like a magician waiting for applause. 'Okay now? Shall we go?'

He sets off without waiting for an answer and Anna, pulling her woollen hat down over her ears to shut out the rush of water and wind, is immediately aware of the throb of pulsing blood inside her head, the prickles of anxiety which tickle her fingertips and toes. Yet they subside as Graham turns and, standing with one foot on a boulder at the side of the footpath, offers her his gloved hand. She walks forward and places her small mittened one in its large fuzzy palm.

He encloses it, and as his fingers tighten she is back walking with her father all those years ago. She remembers holding his hand, only relinquishing it if the walk got too difficult and she needed both her hands for balance. He always carried a stout stick, which had come from Egypt or India or Kenya, depending what story he was telling on that particular occasion. As far as Anna was concerned these inconsistencies (or 'lies' as her mother called them) were a small price to pay for the rare pleasure of his company. The stick was made of light polished wood and had a bird's head carved at one end. The bird's mouth was open in a grotesque kind of grimace, whether of pain or anger it was difficult to say. When her father was away Anna would remove it from the umbrella stand in the hallway, stroke the shiny bird's head with her index finger and poke her little finger into its ridged mouth. On several occasions when her parents had been fighting Anna heard her mother threaten to throw it away along with all the rest of his 'junk', but she had never dared. It was the only thing he took with him when walking. He would twirl it sometimes like a cheerleader's baton or tuck it under his arm like a sergeant-major to make Anna giggle. Sometimes he used it as a walking-stick when he got breathless, occasionally he would use it to prod the ground or overturn some small rock. *What must it be like,* the little girl had wondered, squatting down and peering at the insect life struggling to survive beneath the stone, *to have the lid of your world torn off like that?* What if the sky just opened up and an unimaginably huge wooden tower descended to create chaos out of what had been a settled way of life. She imagined the fear, the sheer blind panic that would ensue as flux replaced certainties and the world appeared limitless.

He encloses it, and she is back at the altar, wrapped from head to toe in spun lace like a white pupa, as the organ throbs and the congregation rustles discreetly behind them. He slides the gold ring on her finger, they repeat words mouthed by the priest in front of them and it is over. Her veil screens the world with its fine gauze mesh and she is reluctant to throw it back, so Graham has to do it. Tenderly, placing each thumb and forefinger at the edge of the net, he lifts it up as if releasing a rare butterfly he has caught.

'Come on daydreamer!' The familiar note of kindly impatience. A tug of her hand. They walk.

For an hour or so the desolation and beauty of the hills take over. It's always the vastness of everything that Anna loves.

'But where does it all end, Daddy?' she demanded on one of their precious walks, when she was only young and her mother was having another bad attack of nerves.

'It doesn't,' he laughed.

Graham takes the lead, measuring regular strides with his long, lean frame slightly hunched over and eyes to the ground for any obstruction, while the much smaller Anna trots to keep up, looking around and above her and consequently stumbling from time to time. She is alert to everything; the heather's taste, the wind's salty smell and the weight of the heavy grey sky. They pass through a hilltop farm; a rusted gate tethered with old rope creaks open on a yard lifeless apart from hens scratting in the dust. Pieces of farm machinery – wild whorls, twists and spikes of metal – look like abandoned engines of war while, amidst dinted churns, upturned crates and unkempt hay bales, a new car gleams incongruously. From within, the distant blare of a television is heard. The grey Yorkshire stone building is impassive. To Anna it resembles a stout old person sitting squarely with arms folded and feet firmly on the ground, refusing to be budged. *I was here first,* it says to her. *You two walk where you like. I'll be here long after you've gone, anyway.*

'I've been told about this marvellous view across the whole of Egton Moor. If we take this path here, then a left fork and follow it for about three quarters of a mile, climbing all the time, I reckon we should be at this vantage point marked on the map.'

'There's a mist falling, Graham.' She hadn't wanted to say anything, had thought round all different ways of saying it without sounding nagging, boring or opinionated and then suddenly had just blurted it out.

There was a fractional pause.

'I am aware of that, Anna. But it's only another three quarters of a mile and I know exactly where we are. It seems a shame to turn back now after we've come all this way.' There is condensation on his beard now and his nose is pink at its tip. Anna thinks how ridiculous and yet how appealing he looks. (That 'damned little boy lost look' as her mother used to say. 'It got me every time.') 'Your mother said she'd give the kids tea. We're in no rush.'

'Oh, let's go on to your stupid vantage point then.'

'Good girl.'

They take what Graham says is their left fork but within ten minutes or so the footpath peters out; there still appears to be a line to follow, or perhaps they see one because they want to. Soon that self-delusion dissolves too. The ground becomes spongy and they both stumble occasionally on grass tussocks. As her hand goes down to stop herself from falling, Anna makes contact with a pile of sheep dung. The black pellets are hard and shake off her palms like berries, but as she brings her hand near her face its smell reminds her of her father's old tweed jacket, the one he always wore when walking. Tobacco, sheep dung and a slight whiff of pubs: whisky and beer. And, just occasionally, the tang of a perfume her mother never used. When her father died, Anna was only ten. Her mother wasn't really deep down sad, she could tell. Certainly she cried a lot and looked miserable, but Anna knew that the lid on her world hadn't been ripped off the way hers had.

The mist now cloaks them. It hoods their heads, hangs on their shoulders, wraps itself around their torsos, clings to their legs. It is Anna's wedding veil and her father's shroud. They should still be climbing but the ground is falling away beneath them, so they edge forward, carefully clinging to one another. At one point Graham's foot sinks into soft mud and he is sinking like the stuff of dreams. Anna helps him haul it out. They are lost. Since they both know that this is a fact, there is little point in discussing it.

'What good does talking do anyway?' Graham had said once. 'It doesn't alter the facts. You just have to go on.' Their bodies are hunched against the wind and they are making little headway.

'Here?' Anna eventually shouts and indicates a pile of boulders to their right. Graham nods his assent and they crouch in the lee, the wind ballooning their cagoules when a gust catches them.

'It'll lift soon!' Graham bellows at her. Anna notices his teeth are chattering, his lips bluish. He fumbles to get the map and peers at it, then takes the compass out from round his neck and shakes it. He needs things to work, systems in place, a set route and destination.

'Can't we just walk?' she'd asked in the early days, 'just walk without knowing where we're going?'

'I can't really see the point in that,' he'd replied, puzzled.

Now she watches, as if from a distance, idly wondering what death out here will be like. A slow drifting away into numbness, then unconsciousness? She burrows further down like a small animal. Her father had died in Cropton Forest, his large frame sprawled on a carpet of pine needles, his stick lying at some distance from him as if a sceptre hurled by some avenging, mythical God.

'Did he...?' she'd asked the doctor and he, misunderstanding, had replied:

'No, he didn't suffer. Heart attack.'

She couldn't then bring herself to complete the question, asking if he thought her father would have seen some scrap of sky through the canopy of huge trees before he went.

'Just look at that damned sky!' he used to urge her, brandishing the stick at it like a modern day Lear. 'Bloody incredible!'

And they'd watch a grey scudding sky over Wheeldale Moor, or one so blue it hurt your eyes from the top of the steps by Whitby Abbey. Two days after the funeral her mother had given his jacket and stick to Oxfam. When Anna found out, she had pedalled furiously down to the shop but they had already been sold, and for the first time she cried, great raw sobs which tore at her throat and contorted her face in front of the two horrified old ladies doing their once-fortnightly voluntary work. Unable to stem the flow of tears, they'd called her mother who, resentful at no longer having a monopoly on public demonstrations of grief, took her straight away to see the family doctor.

'Where does it hurt, Anna?' he'd enquired gently, feeling her hot forehead, her racing pulse. 'Just tell me where it hurts.'

Unable to speak, she'd simply placed a hand over her heart.

Anna thinks that maybe they should get up and move. Her watch shows four o'clock, proper darkness will be here soon. But Graham has gone still, so she chafes his hands just like she wished she'd been able to with her father. She is calm, content even. Not that she wants him to die, not that she wants to die herself for that matter. It is, after all, unlikely. They are both young and fit, not too far from civilisation and their parked car will be a sure sign to someone that they are in trouble. Dying must be a lot better when it's done with someone you love anyway. If you can live, and die, with the weaknesses and faults and imperfections then that's all that matters. That's what she'd been so angry about, so angry that she had never shed a tear at the funeral, just felt an overwhelming rage against a world and a woman that had let him take his last walk alone.

But now the mist is lifting. Standing up and stretching, she can see a little more clearly, she is sure. It's like doing one of those magic drawings when you rub your pencil over what is apparently a blank page and slowly but surely a picture starts to emerge.

A stunted, blackened tree.

A woman who craved the comfort of a man who was always home just for her, who liked the warm fug of the inside and distrusted open spaces.

A couple of sheep pushing their grubby fleeces up against one another.

A woman who needed a father for her angry, confused young daughter.

A footpath only about twenty yards to the right.

A daughter who resented this replacement and who later married a man she mistakenly thought resembled her father.

Anna realises they have come to a near circle. She can just make out the outline of their car, and the stream glinting like a slug's trail in the valley below. It is finally time to leave her father and make her own way back.

'Graham, Graham!' She shakes him hard now – he comes to, and struggles to his feet. 'Let's get going. It's late and it's getting cold.'

'What?' He is bad-tempered and stiff-limbed, rebuffing her offers of help like a dog shaking off water. 'I must have dropped off. What time is it? Whose idea was it to stop? We should have carried on. What a bloody shambles. That's the last time I come walking in this fucking place. Compass was knackered. Useless map as well. Don't know where the hell we are.'

'It's okay, I know.'

'You do?'

She nods.

'That's alright then.' He looks at her fiercely. 'And what

exactly are you smiling at me like that for?'

Anna takes her husband's hand in hers. 'Come on, you. We're going home.'

Under a leaden carapace of sky the two figures pick their way down the hill, the smaller leading.

# Seeing the Light

She had a son called Ben who was her third child and he was a stain, ugly and rust-coloured, which seeped through the thin protective membrane of her being and was immovable. She cherished him the way you cherish an imperfection, a blemish on the otherwise smooth skin of her life. Ben developed into the child no-one wanted around, the child with whom other parents favourably compared their own. He destroyed possessions, both his own and others, and underwent mood swings that were sudden and violent. He hated with venom but became passionately absorbed in people and things too. The greatest miracle, as far as she was concerned, was that she went on loving him despite it all, defending the indefensible, unintentionally spinning a cocoon of care and concern around the two of them that excluded others.

One scorching summer's day, when Ben was about five, the two of them stood outside the house waiting for the rest of the family to leave for a day out in Scarborough. For what seemed like hours a welter of buckets, spades, towels, beachballs, deckchairs and holdalls had mounted in the hallway. The carpet became gritty underfoot from last year's sand and the dank, fishy smell of seaweed hung on the air. Ben had refused to go. He hated the noise of the seaside. He was frightened of seagulls, donkeys, amusement arcades and waves and so she had said she might as well stay with him. Simon shrugged, her other two boys pulled faces and then returned to their dispute about the relative merits of North or South Bay. Yet Ben resented them going and melded his body into her side, whimpering like a small animal as she made sandwiches and divided them into three neat parcels. Eventually, the car was loaded. Squinting her eyes against the angry sun, with each banging of a door, the car seemed to swell in front of her until it became one large metallic carapace oozing sweat and the smell of plastic. The children pushed their faces up against the glass until they were distorted in order to frighten Ben. She scolded, soothed and exchanged essential information and a dry brush of the lips with her husband. Finally he backed slowly down the drive. Leaning out of the windows and banging the sides of the car, the children screeched with excitement while Ben blocked his ears against the noise. As the dust settled back on the driveway, the two of them stood in silence feeling the beat of the sun on their heads. In the distance she could hear a lawnmower, the creak of a swing, a radio.

He wanted to make a lantern. He'd seen one made on a children's television programme and wanted to copy it. She felt the familiar knotting feeling in her belly. Memories of other failed projects were scorched in her mind – the lopsided Christmas fairy they'd made, resulting in him pulling the tree down; their chocolate cake that had hit the kitchen wall like some slapstick pantomime scene. The shouts, tears, mess, recriminations. She started to suggest other alternative activities but one glance at his closed-down face and she knew it was useless. Anyway, it was too hot to argue.

They'd gone down to the shed at the bottom of the orchard and found some withies she'd once got for a basket-making class she'd quickly had to abandon when Ben refused to go to bed without her there. They soaked them in the old rainwater barrel to make them supple, then bent them into petal shapes and bound them with gaffer tape. He wanted paper on them, thin paper, and impatiently rooting around in the cool darkness of the box room, she'd found large sheets of pale pink tissue paper inside an otherwise empty shirt box. Sitting back on her heels and holding up to the light one of the gauzy sheets, she saw again her pink-smudged wedding day; in an orchard bulging with apple blossom, rows of trestle tables covered with crisp white damask cloths, overlaid with sheets of pink tissue; fine Georgian silver, pink roses in silver bowls, soft pink cones of serviettes. There had been so much left over: food, drink, presents, the paper. She drew the paper towards her and smoothed the sheet back over her face so that her lips and nose splayed in a grotesque salmon-coloured mask. A shout bought her back to the present. Grabbing the rest of the paper she hurried back outside.

Painstakingly, they stretched the paper between the frames until taut. From time to time it would get a crease or would tear slightly from being pulled too tightly. By mutual consent it was scrunched up, an abandoned rose, and another oval of paper carefully cut out. They sat in the long grass, totally absorbed in what they were doing. There were wasps after fallen overripe fruit but the two of them were immune. They both wore floppy white hats and their faces, arms and knees became daubed with the white sticky paste they were using. Lunch and tea were snacks she bought outside on trays and he, normally so greedy with his food, had barely touched any of it. After lunch he'd fallen asleep for an hour or so and she'd moved him into the shade where the light dappled his smooth young skin, stained with paste, grass and food.

At the end of the afternoon they'd made enough petals and could fasten them together, three layers of them, the different sizes inverted to form a huge fairylike scallop. A candle in a jar and a long pole for holding and carrying completed the creation, and she told Ben they would light it when it was dark to get the full effect of the lantern's beauty. He would have his supper and bath and then she would light it. But he wanted the light now. No, later. Why? Because it'll be better then. Why? Because it will be darker. I want it now. Later. Now. Later.

She left him kicking and screaming while she went inside to fetch him a glass of juice. Often tantrums were eased by administering food or drink. She poured Ribena out, taking pleasure in the heavy purple liquid sliding down the side of the glass. The pipes groaned as she turned on the tap in the kitchen and she thought of where she would display the lantern for the others when they returned. She would hang it in the porch, turn off all the downstairs lights and they would see it illuminated as they came up the drive, a beacon of her achievement. She imagined how she would casually describe to Simon the time she and Ben had spent on its construction; how he would have to be impressed by his youngest son's creativity and patience; how she and him could for once unite in parental admiration. Once Ben was settled, perhaps they could have a meal, just the two of them, with candles, wine and soft lights. And afterwards, perhaps they might make love. A thin runnel of sweat trickled between her breasts and she pressed her groin once, twice, against the cold, hard edge of the sink. With a spasm from the tap, water gushed over the top of the glass. Smiling, she poured a little out and went back into the garden.

He had raped it. Every petal had been punched in. Shreds of tissue paper hung limply in surrender from the frame which stood balanced awkwardly on one side like the skeleton of a massacred animal. The jam jar was smashed, the pole snapped in two. He'd even wrenched some of the withies apart, though, lying on the ground, they still clung to their curves as if ashamed of their violation. He stood by the debris, half defiant and half afraid. He was panting, his cheeks were flushed and there was a dark stain on the front of his shorts.

'Mu...m.' A cry of despair, of fear.

'It doesn't matter.'

Then, defeated, she slumped down onto the grass and cried. The crying took a long time, but then again it had waited a long time. It was not just for the broken lantern but for her broken dreams, for the futility of it all and the exhausting struggle to keep everything together, everything taut. She remembered the pleading look on Simon's face after he'd done it, while she still lay there in a tangle of skewed clothes and sticky dampness. How she'd felt, bizarrely, a need to protect him, to bend around him like the pliant withies and corral his anger.

'I'm so sorry...'

'It doesn't matter.'

'Can we still...?'

'Of course we can.'

A fairytale wedding, a pink and white confection of hope, followed by ten years and three boys. More than many others had. And yet. She shifted position. An apple had leaked its brown mushy ripeness onto her skirt. Ben had moved a little distance away and had squatted down with his back turned. Afterwards, Simon had sat on the side of the bed, leaning forwards with his head in his hands and she'd run her hand down his spine. It doesn't matter.

The air turned cool, the leaves started whispering and the ground breathed up its evening moistness. The two of them were still there when the others returned later in the evening to find the house in darkness, no meal cooked and no willing arms for wet clothes, towels and remains of the picnic. Simon was irritated, expecting praise for what he perceived as his Herculean efforts and disappeared inside, pointedly snapping on lights everywhere. The other two children stepped on the detritus of cane, tape and paper as they excitedly told of the castle, the cliff cable car, the lighthouse and proffered their tacky spoils of candyfloss and lollies.

He'd just wanted to see the light, he'd told her later, as she tucked the white sheets round his rigid little body and kissed him goodnight. She wouldn't let him see the light and he'd wanted to. He'd wanted to see the light. See the light. The light. His dark, troubled eyes held hers for the merest flicker of time and then he heaved onto his side, away from her. She reached for the switch of the bedside lamp and, in the moment before darkness swallowed them both, she saw he had clutched tightly in one hand his present from the seaside – a giant baby's dummy in lurid red sugar.

# Animal House

George was going to see the animals. Tonight. *Scooby dooby doo, where are you.* He had to be careful, very careful. They weren't allowed up there. Shorty had got as far as the entrance before he was caught and then he was in big trouble. Slap around the head, slap on the back of the legs, jab in the ribs. *Pinch, punch first of the month and no returns.* They shouldn't hit them and Shorty, being Shorty, tried to complain but then things started to go missing from his locker and he got small portions of grub and Shorty really liked his grub so he shut up pretty quick.

After lights out George lay very still and rigid beneath the rough grey blanket and white sheet. Usually he rubbed the darns in the sheet between his fingers and thumb seeing how quickly he could make a hole. Mind you, if he did it too fast he'd rub the skin off the tips of his fingers and they'd bleed. He always howled at the sight of his own blood, so then someone would come and shush and tut and give him a spoonful of sticky pink stuff which sent him into a shuddering sleep. No rubbing tonight though. Or playing with his John Thomas either. No sirree. Tonight he imagined he was a mummy, bound from head to foot in bandages.

*Where's my mummy?*
*Gone away.*
*Where am I going to?*
*A place you'll be looked after.*

Sickly moonlight filtered through the thin institutional curtains and spattered on the floor. George pulled his covers aside and swung his legs out, reaching for a puddle of light. His bare feet stuck to the lino and, as he crept round hunting for slippers, his skin made little tearing noises like plasters being ripped off. At last he found the naughty slippers which had hidden themselves under his bed – *finders keepers losers weepers* – and carefully put them on. Then he wrapped his Spiderman dressing gown around him and at last was ready to go. Along the corridor, which as per usual stunk something dreadful of pee and farty sprouts, down the back stairs on tippy toe as quiet as a mouse and out of the small side door next to the kitchens. *Easey-peasey lemon squeezy.* It smelt nice outside: of grass and earth. He bent down and scooped up a handful of soil and sniffed it like a doggy. So good. But the animals, he was going to see the animals, he'd better get going. This was really going to be something to tell the others the next day.

He trotted confidently through the network of paths that he knew would take him to the animals' house. It was a new building set apart from the rest at the top of a gentle hill. Even at some distance he could hear their noise, a throbbing and pounding which made him so excited that he had to stop and dive into some bushes and have a pee. It ended up as only a dribble but if he'd been caught doing that in the daytime he'd really have copped it. Probably have had to sit on the chair in the corner with his trousers around his ankles so that everyone could laugh at him. *Little Jack Horner...* he didn't like people laughing at him. Shaking drips off his winkle because he definitely didn't want damp jimmy bottoms, he looked back at the view behind him. Chestnuts, the house where he lived, was the biggest of them all. Funny how they were called houses because they weren't really houses at all. He could just remember his proper house, where he and Mam had lived. Nobody else had lived there, just them. At Chestnuts there were loads of people and everything was massive like in *Alice in Wonderland*. The pot for their tea was a huge metal one, so huge that it took two people to lift it when full. From the front, Chestnuts looked really grand like all the other houses. They'd been built a long time ago, the stone was that powerful grey stuff and they had pillars and even turrets on some of them. But if you went round the back, where all the dustbins and fire escapes and dirty laundry were, you saw it differently. One of his few memories was of going to see a pantomime. He'd sat through it open-mouthed, caught up in the magic of the princess's fairy castle. Then afterwards for some reason they'd gone round backstage, and he'd seen how it was all make-believe and how the scenery was rather tatty close to and propped up from behind, and he'd screamed and kicked in rage and Mam had been upset and cried all the way home on the bus.

A sudden blast of noise from the animals' house made him realise he shouldn't be hanging about. They weren't always there, and besides, he was getting cold. He hurried along, puffing slightly as he climbed the hill, drawing nearer and nearer to his goal. Then all at once it seemed he was there at the gate and nervous because he hadn't worked out what he would do next. But he couldn't go back, so if he couldn't go back he had to go on. And when he knew that he *had* to go on, he had no choice anymore, which made him very sad. Instantly he realised that whatever he did it would be wrong and he'd be in trouble – it'd turn out just like before and he just hoped there wouldn't be too much blood because he hated the sight of blood, especially his own. So he opened the gate and walked up the short path to the door, and opened that too and then he was inside.

They must have to keep it hot for the animals because a wave of heat hit him in the face. The smell was damp and stale rather like the hamster cage back at Chestnuts. There was screeching and calling and the thump, thump, thump of the noise. And as he wandered into the main enclosure he was suddenly surrounded by the wild creatures who leapt and shook and made strange jerky movements with their limbs and contorted their faces at one another. Coloured straw at their feet was occasionally kicked up by their crazed actions and lay strewn across the area. A baboon with a large red face and hairy chest operated the noise from a raised platform, encouraging the animals to writhe by uttering a mixture of squeals and shouts. A group in one corner – they were zebras because of their stripy tops – were emptying drinks over each other and braying, while in another snakes wrapped themselves around each other's slithery bodies. There was food over at one side but the animals must have fought over it because it was all mixed up and messy and a lot of it was on the ground and being trodden in. There was one creature, a parrot because she had lots of shiny different colours, who seemed to be the most important one. She had a badge on with a number four and a nought. George knew what that meant because that was his locker number and it was really nice to see something he recognised. Of course that made everything not so strange and gave a reason for him being there so, hardly noticing that the noise had stopped and the creatures were much quieter, he rushed up to the parrot, pushed his face up near to hers and, grabbing the badge, tried to explain how good it was that she had this number.

Then he was on the floor, *Georgy Porgy pudding and pie kissed the girls and made them cry, when the boys came out to play...* but he couldn't run away. He was held down by strong arms, it took four of them to hold him down because he was big, and the faces above him were red and angry. All of a sudden he knew he was going to cack his pants and he tried to explain but they just held him down even more firmly. Then he blubbed, he knew he was being a baby, *cry baby cry baby*, but he couldn't help it, and snot ran down into his mouth like it always did when he blubbed and he couldn't get a hanky. The parrot was upset, he could see that, especially when he couldn't hold his bum cheeks together any longer and the shit came out and soiled his jimmies. The smell was awful, too, which it always was after shepherd's pie the day before because the meat they used wasn't nice meat. She was crying, and he remembered Mam crying before she went away, and he felt as if his heart would break because it had been him that had made them both cry like that. His fault.

Then they must have felt sorry for him because they let him get up off the floor and one of the zebras took him to the toilet so he could clean his bum and wash his hands. Someone else gave him some trousers, but they were too big so he looked like a clown. When he got back they'd fetched him some food and a fizzy drink, which tasted a bit sour, but which he drank so they'd stay not angry with him. Then they fetched him another, in a bigger glass this time, so he drank that too. A paper hat was placed on his head, some coloured straw around his neck and George heard himself laughing loudly. He was having such a good time he never wanted to leave.

So when they came from Chestnuts to get him and try and make him put the horrible jacket on, he was mad. Very mad. He fought his keepers, fought like a tiger. Kicked. Spat. Growled. His dressing gown fell open, one sleeve of his his jimmy jacket got ripped and he lost a slipper. He couldn't stop blubbing, although now it was angry fierce sobs that hurt his chest. Half-dragging and half-pushing, the two of them got him as far as the door, but there was a group of creatures in the way so one of the keepers asked them to move, saying something about an animal. Exhausted, George went limp and dropped his head – *sticks and stones may break my bones but words will never hurt me* – and when he raised it there was Mam with a blotchy tear marked face.

'Sorry,' he said. 'I didn't mean to...'

The rest was drowned out by a sudden blast of the noise restarting. Mam tried to say something to the keepers, she was upset again, but this time he knew that it was not at him but for him. She wagged her finger and then put her hands on her hips like she used to do when he was bullied. Just for a brief moment he felt the keepers' grip on his arms relax as they tried to reply to her, and at the same time there was a surge of creatures coming through the doorway from the other side. They were in a single line, each one holding onto the other so that they looked like a giant caterpillar; as the caterpillar weaved past, separating Mam and the keepers, hands reached out and pulled George in. His waist was clamped from behind and he had to reach forward to the creature in front in order to keep his balance. Then he was part of the chain, one of them. As it coiled around the main enclosure, more and more creatures joined in until at last all were caught. *Ring a ring of rosies a pocket full of posies.* The caterpillar's tail whiplashed the keepers who, with waving arms, were in pursuit. *We all fall down.* The caterpillar kicked its legs out either side in time to the beat. George felt the noise enter his body through the soles of his feet and travel upwards until it exploded out through his ears. He turned his face upwards to the roof and gave a great howl of joy. As if on cue, bars of pure white light began to flash and the brown-skinned caterpillar, trapped in its violet edged cage, twitched and jerked uncontrollably just like George did after one of his treatments.

*We all fall down.*
   *We all fall down.*
      *We all fall down.*

# Reflections

Childhood memories? I don't think I have any really, only the fire. I can remember birthdays, Christmas, school, all the usual sort of things but nothing that marks me out from everyone else. Only the fire. Even now it's so vivid to me that I think it's somehow wiped out all the rest.

I must have been about ten. We lived in Cornwall in this huge house virtually on the edge of a cliff... it's funny to look back on the inverted snobbery a lot of children have. I was so ashamed of it, would much rather have been down on the council estate where the rest of the village kids lived. Anyway, I slept up at the top of the house in the attic. That sounds awful, as if I was shut away by cruel parents! It was actually very comfortable, I liked the feeling of being high up and I had all the room I wanted for my collections. It also kept me clear of Cathy, who was only five then, and the new baby. Not that I was jealous. I never liked people fussing round me, touching and so on, and I knew I looked and acted much older than my years. They called me The Prof at school because I spent my breaks and dinner hours alone in the library rather than skylarking with the rest of them in the playground.

Yes, my Granny was someone special to me. Of course now, with hindsight, I realise she was rather eccentric, especially in those days. She rode a motorbike well into her seventies and wore trousers, shirts and baggy cardigans like a man. She chain-smoked too – always had a cigarette gripped between her teeth at the side of her mouth so she could talk at the same time. Again, it didn't register then but I think she probably drank a lot. My mother disapproved, I could tell that by the way she would press her lips together tightly whenever Granny sloshed a generous measure from the dark green bottle into her tumbler, topped it with tonic and plopped in two ice cubes from the silver and walnut barrel.

'Cheerio, chaps, down the hatch!' she'd say and wink at me behind my mother's back.

Our best times were spent outside at the bonfire. In a corner of the paddock she'd rake great piles of damp leaves and undergrowth, while I dragged over all manner of fallen branches and debris. She muttered to herself continuously, my father used to say that's where I got my habit from, often using words I instinctively knew to be rude without ever to my knowledge having heard them before. Then, when we were both satisfied with our heap, Granny would take a box of matches from the droopy pocket of her cardigan and strike one. That was always a magic moment for me and despite all her odd ways, you know, she would never allow me to light the fire. She would crouch down, me at her side, and gently touch the tip to the scrumpled-up balls of newspaper that she'd stuffed in underneath. As if hypnotised, I would stare at the flicker of blue and yellow tongue whose tentative licking promised the ecstasy of the full blaze, the crackling, fighting glory that was the fire. I'd only move away when the intensity of the heat made my skin tingle and eyes water. Sometimes, fancifully, I'd imagine it as a funeral pyre for all my bad thoughts and feelings. It was a sort of private ceremony, and once, when Cathy had come toddling out into the garden to investigate, Granny had kindly but firmly taken her back indoors so there were just the two of us. Then we'd stand or sit, Granny's arm around me, and watch – watch until all that remained was a heap of ash which winked red at you when raked through. Sometimes she'd bring marshmallows and we'd impale then on sticks and push them into the embers, where they became encrusted with black flakes but with a sticky white goo inside that burnt the roof of your mouth.

Granny died just after we moved down to Cornwall and before the baby was born. I believe it was from a fall. My mother and father went back for the funeral and we were left with the au-pair. I wasn't a child given to great shows of emotion, that's still true of me today, but I do remember feeling angry that I wasn't allowed to go and say a proper goodbye to Granny. To punish them I made sure the au-pair walked out shortly after they returned. Then about three months later my mother had the baby, another girl, and about that time I can recall overhearing a conversation between my parents.

They were in the nursery and must have been looking at the baby. She said, I can't remember the exact words, but something about how she was glad it had been a girl because that way one new life had replaced an old one. Standing behind the door listening to this, I dug my nails into my palms with such intensity that the indentations remained there for some days. To talk about my beloved Granny in that way – as if she could be replaced by the unpleasant, wailing little scrap who they both worshipped. I so missed Granny – the rough wool of her cardigan chafing against my cheek, her large, nicotined, oily hands that ruffled my hair and gripped my shoulders and the woody, smoky smell that impregnated her clothes, skin and hair, and was to me a sweet perfume.

The fire happened in the Autumn following her death. I don't know the exact date. In the early hours of the morning I was woken by my mother's shouts. Never a deep sleeper, I jumped out of bed and saw a tiny wisp of smoke curl under my door. At first I thought... they're trying to smoke me out... you know how you have these totally irrational reactions when you've been woken up unexpectedly. Then I came to my senses, pulled on my dressing-gown and made my way down to the first floor, slowly because the thick acrid smoke was stinging my eyes. From downstairs I could hear shouting and breaking glass. On the landing I met my mother who was holding Cathy by the hand. My little sister's face was puffy and pink from sleep while our mother, stripped of her customary poise, looked like a wild thing. Her dark hair, usually so elegantly coiled in a chignon, was streaming loose like a witch's and her pale face was daubed with smuts and smudges like a soldier's camouflage. She grabbed my arm,

'Richard! Take Cathy, go downstairs and get outside through the French windows in the dining-room. Daddy has broken them open. Mind the glass. I'm going to... Oh God!' She broke off as a huge explosion ripped the air apart and a muffled noise came from my father down below. I could see she was torn between staying with us and going to him. She hesitated, her mouth slack, almost staggered then turned and rushed to the main stairs calling over her shoulder. 'Go on Richard! Move!'

Trailing a now-snivelling Cathy, I cautiously felt my way down. I could hear the crackle of flames but had yet to see the fire. There was only the smoke, a grey shroud which veiled everything familiar. I kept rubbing my eyes, as if by doing so I could wipe it away like a dirty mark on my glasses. Actually, it's funny but polishing my glasses when they are perfectly clean is still a habit of mine.

When we reached the bottom of the stairs I caught sight of myself in the large gilded mirror that hung in the entrance hall. We had a lot of mirrors in our house, always had done, as I think my mother was rather vain and enjoyed checking on her appearance as she moved around the place. Sometimes she would stop in front of the glass with Cathy or the baby in her arms and adjust her expression, play with it, until she had achieved what she wanted. Before going out to dinner my father and her would stand in front of it, pose, and then laugh and nuzzle their heads together. Myself, I never looked if I

could help it, only do now if it's absolutely necessary –
checking my tie is straight, that kind of thing. But, as I was
saying, at that particular moment I did look. The reflected
image was a misty one; the heat had caused condensation and
the droplets looked like tears on the face. That gave me a bit of
a jolt, I can tell you, as I never used to cry so it was like seeing
myself as someone else if that makes any sense. And somehow
it made me remember what I had to do – it was really very
simple – go back and rescue the baby. The explosion was from
the central heating oil-tank in an outhouse just off the kitchen,
and the nursery was above it.

Acting quickly, I led Cathy through the dining room, lifting
her over the glass fragments that littered the floor by the
windows and dumping her on the damp grass outside. She
started to wail of course but I managed to quieten her with the
same threat I always used. Then I look a deep lungful of the
sharp night air and returned indoors. Creeping up the
staircase I found my way to the nursery and stood over her
cot. She was still sleeping soundly, just giving an occasional
husky dry cough. I looked down at her – they'd given her
Granny's name, did I mention that before? – thought for a
moment, then scooped her up in my arms, all the time holding
her as far away from my body as possible because I never
liked that sweet powdery smell that clings to babies. It still
makes me feel sick. Leaving the nursery, I caught sight of the
tiny picture on the wall by the door. My picture. It was of a
little boy in an old-fashioned white nightshirt holding his
hands up to a starry night sky with the caption 'Little Hands
Outstretched To Bless'. It had always hung in my bedroom at
Granny's where I stayed when my parents were away on their
many trips abroad.

'When I'm a goner,' she used to say, 'everything in this
room will be yours, Rich.'

But they'd said I was a big boy now, too old for baby

pictures. I slipped it into my pocket.

I met my mother on the stairs, and the look on her face when she saw me was all I could have wanted.

'Oh thank God! She's safe. Give her to me darling and let's get outside. Daddy has done all he can but it's hopeless. The fire brigade should be here any moment.'

As if on cue, we both heard the distant sirens, and a few minutes later we were all outside standing on the lawn, watching the hoses snaking out from the massive red machines that stood panting on the forecourt. Water jetted into the right wing of the house, solid columns that pounded the building till only black smoke belched from the windows.

By the time it was all over, Cathy had somehow managed to end up sitting inside one of the engines with a fireman's hat on, her cheeks bulging with toffees; my mother, having recovered her composure and tidied herself up, stood proudly next to my father who was seemingly the hero of the occasion having fought the fire single-handedly and prevented its spread. Blackened almost beyond recognition, his bare torso glistening with sweat, he was laughingly brushing aside praise and talking of 'generous insurance cover'. My mother, all the time rocking the baby in her arms, looked up at him with an adoring look that should have been for me.

It was then – rather melodramatically, really – finding myself distanced from the family, I took out the picture from my dressing-gown pocket, placed it carefully on the ground and smashed it with a stone I'd taken from the rockery, grinding my feet into the glass until it fragmented into thousands of crystal splinters. Picking it up, I shook them off and took out the print. It was only thin and flimsy and I was pleased that the little boy got wrinkles all over him as I crumpled it up. Next, from my other pocket I took out my special box of matches and struck one. I crouched down and put the tip of the match to the print. It was a sweet moment and, watching the picture burn, I felt that I had at least partly done what I had set out to.

What else do I remember? I think that's about it. Oh yes, I had to go to hospital to get my feet stitched up, that didn't make me very popular! The fire was on the local news because of the suspected arson, and I was a minor celebrity at school for a few days but it was all forgotten much sooner than I'd hoped. The damaged part of the house was gutted, then rebuilt and we moved a year or so later. I think my father probably made a fair old profit.

So there was no lasting harm done; that's why I can't understand why I still have these nightmares. And every time it's the same. I'm looking into a mirror and staring back at me is a little boy with outstretched hands, each one holding a lighted match. There's a caption underneath the mirror but I can never quite make it out. The boy is crying but the tears are tiny pieces of glass, and as they slide down his face they leave trickles of blood. I suppose it's quite natural to have dreams like that, after all it was a pretty traumatic experience for a young child; it's just the way they keep recurring after all this time. I sometimes feel that I'm trying to punish myself for something. How's that for a bit of amateur psychoanalysis!

Anyway, I can see my time is almost up for this week so I'd better be thinking of making tracks. Thank you. It does me good to talk to someone. There's no one at work who has the time or inclination to listen, and I don't keep in close touch with the family. My parents have retired, moved back to the West Country, and Cathy's married with children of her own. You know, it's difficult to accept that my mother is a granny herself now. I prefer to remember her that night of the fire – wild, distracted yet still beautiful – momentarily clinging to me for support. The memories of my own Granny are so faded and brittle they crumble if I handle them too much. Yes, at times I feel she is there in the dreams, although I never actually see her.

And sometimes I even believe she was there beside me that night, encouraging me, as I crouched down and lit the match.

My other sister? That was very sad. She died shortly after we moved to Cornwall. A terrible accident. Toddling, she tripped and fell into an open fire. She was so badly burned she died on the way to hospital. I was there and saw it happen. There was absolutely nothing I could do to stop it. Absolutely nothing. I have felt that my mother blamed me for it happening – she's never actually said anything, but then no one ever really does, do they? That's why I prefer my own company. A lot of time I spend reading, and on my stamp and coin collections. What I really love doing is crouching in front of my own fire at home, just staring into it and imagining pictures in the flames. You can create whole new worlds for yourself. This will sound absurd, but often I see Granny and my little sister, dancing and burning side by side, and if I get my face close enough it's as if her hot, frightened breath is right up against my cheek. Both of them beckon me in, holding out their streaming, fiery arms as if to embrace me.

I sometimes think it's the only touch I could bear.

# Double Vision

'Runt, runt!' the kids would jeer as Jacko darted, skipped and weaved through the straggling groups making their way up the school drive. I don't know if they knew what 'runt' meant; perhaps they just liked the sound of the woody word that was so much like the c one. At any rate, they were right about his size – he was small, very small, and he had a habit of thrusting one shoulder and then the other forward and up as if trying to jolt himself into growth. He was also dirty, but not with the kind of dirt that makes so many little boys endearing; this was engrained, etched into his palms, his neck, his knees. The smell that this kind of encrusted grime exuded was stale but rather sweet.

Jacko was cross-eyed and short-sighted and it was difficult to believe that the flimsy pair of specs, taped over the bridge where they were regularly broken in fights, could remedy either of these defects. He would bark rather than talk at you, asking questions, continually demanding, and the questions would pin you, hold you and Jacko would have what he craved more than anything – your attention. Like a scruffy performing monkey, Jacko would do anything for attention. He was rumoured to have eaten a bowl of dog food for a bet, although it was quite possible that hunger played a part too.

I started work just after Christmas. Jacko's Year 11 class consisted of twenty boys and four girls, the latter for the most part being the butt of sexual innuendo from the boys. Most of them were not taking any exams and faced an uninspiring future; even worse than being overtly aggressive and disruptive, they were cynically resigned to what lay ahead. Occasionally they turned to Jacko for entertainment...

'Go on Jacko, you tell 'er'

'He's a fuckin' nutter, Jacko is!'

For the most part the class and I enjoyed a mutual tolerance. Jacko was a different matter. He was adept at spotting weakness, prodding it, rubbing at it until it erupted. For much of the time I hated him; at times I could feel the fury starting upwards from the pit of my stomach and I knew I needed to vent this violence. I'd felt the same way towards my own child at times, wanting to hurt, to pull, to punish. Normally, the one part of myself that remained sane and rational ensured the release was exacted on a chair, a door or something similar. But this one day was to be different.

If Jacko had one undisputed talent it was for mimicry. There had been an attempt in the past by a young, hopelessly enthusiastic teacher, naively sure that all social barriers could be broken down, to channel this ability into the school drama group but, not unexpectedly, it failed. The gentle, cultured atmosphere of the latter had been alien to Jacko and he to it. Their cruelty was subtle – no shouts of 'runt' here – middle class courtesy was as engrained in them as Jacko's dirt. However, it was the slight wrinkling of the nose, barely noticeable, as he passed or the quick glance downwards at his battered gym-shoes that gave them away; he was not one of them and the free-thinking, free-wheeling Drama Group (Meets Mondays 3:45 Room 7 – Come Along and Do Your Own Thing) bought their shutters down firmly. Jacko, for his part, mimicked them in an accurate and deadly way, capturing their self-conscious posturing exactly.

'Gayboys', his unequivocal opinion of them.

On this particular occasion it was as if Jacko had intuitively sensed that my spirits were ragged. Earlier that morning, my son Chris and I had clawed and torn at each other's feelings in the way that only people who are close to each other can do. I don't remember what had actually sparked it off – perhaps an untidy room, or a missing sock, or a stain on the carpet – and anyway, it doesn't matter. Both of us would seize on that kind of domestic niggle as fuel for the resentment and anger that were never far from the surface. It was tempting, sometimes useful, to attribute these scenes to the pressures of being on my own but I never quite convinced myself. Jacko, not surprisingly, came from a single-parent family too, but that no more explained his neglect than did his address or his height or his name. In fact, there were some physical similarities between Jacko and Chris. Naturally Chris was clean and well cared for, nothing wrong with his eyesight either, but they were about the same size despite Chris being the younger. There was something about the look they both fixed one with, the look that instilled guilt and inadequacy, that was belligerent and at the same time supplicatory.

'What on earth do you mean?' Chris's father had exploded impatiently when, several months earlier, I had attempted to explain this to him. As he spoke, he was packing things into the big brown battered case which had accompanied us on all the family holidays. Another business trip. More time when Chris and I would be caged together. 'You're always going on about looks and feelings and atmospheres. Always analysing and probing and questioning. Why can't you just take life as it comes and enjoy it?'

'Like you do, I suppose,' I'd retorted bitterly. 'Look, I'm simply trying to make you see how explosive it is here. Chris puts all the pressure on me and it should be on you as well.'

'I can't help being away a lot of the time. What do you expect me to do? Give up my job and we'll live off your income?'

'No, of course not, but sometimes I'm afraid that...'

'It's eight o'clock and I've got to go.' He snapped the case closed and swung it off the bed. 'Look, Chris is fit and happy.

He's got friends, he's doing well at school and he's got his football. Okay, so you have rows but I'm sure that's the same with all teenagers. I must go, I'll ring you tonight.'

It was very shortly after this that he had left us for good. Then I was ill for a while, and the tension had eased between Chris and I. But now, this morning, we had reached the brink once more.

'God, call yourself a mother!' He was standing at the front door, sports bag over his shoulder, playing with the latch but unwilling to go.

'Don't speak to me like that! Who do you think you are? Show some respect.'

'Respect is earned, not yours by right.'

'Very clever, aren't you?'

'You're proud of my ability when it suits you.'

'I'm not proud of you right now, Chris.'

'Snap.' He fixed me with that clear challenging look and I had to turn away.

So when I walked into the classroom that morning, it was a few moments before I fully realised what was going on. I entered the room from the back, by way of a large store cupboard that linked my room with another – not my usual way and obviously not expected. Jacko was entertaining the class, who were sitting around on desks and leaning against the windows, by doing a superb and deadly impersonation of me. All my idiosyncrasies were laid bare – the twiddling with an earring, the repeated use of 'Right then, folks' as a prelude to anything I had to say, my slightly pigeon-toed walk – everything. It was like suddenly catching sight of oneself in a large mirror in a shop, for a split-second not knowing who it is, and then having a swamping realisation of the truth. That was not all. To the obvious delight of the class, Jacko was also repeating an anecdote I had told them the previous week. We had been doing some work on the topic of 'The Family' and I had recounted some insignificant but amusing tale of Chris as a little boy. It had been a good lesson, most of them had swapped stories and there had been laughter, though Jacko had not said anything.

Now in a couple of steps I was at Jacko's shoulder while he, unaware, was still in mid-performance. All that I could grasp was that a grotesque parody of myself was being enacted for cheap entertainment. I suppose my vanity was dented, but there was anger too at how this little boy could hurt me. His use of my story was like a violation of my son somehow, as if Jacko was the dark, negative side of my son. Perhaps a psychologist would explain my actions as revenge against the whole of the male sex, as retribution for the wrongs done to me by little boys who had become older. Be that as it may, I certainly did not think about what I did. I simply slapped him on the side of his face, and as he yelped and ducked, I slapped him again. They didn't amount to much more than taps, but when I stopped I was panting and my heart was racing. Jacko had darted behind a desk and squinted up at me, and whether it was Chris's face or Jacko's I don't know because I was crying. It was over very quickly; the rest of the class had sheepishly found their way back to their places and were half-heartedly getting out books, papers and folders. As for Jacko, he just stood there, one little shoulder thrust forward and a grubby hand rubbing at the side of his head. His expression was difficult to make out.

'Christ, you don't 'alf pack a punch, miss, there's a bloody lump coming up on me 'ead. I could sprag on 'yer and you'd get the push. Yer not meant to clout us anymore. And me specs have bust again.'

Strangely, that was the worst moment of all, for his tone made clear what he felt and what his expression had been. Although complaining because it was expected of him, he actually admired and even respected me because I had behaved the same way as all the other adults in his life had done. He now understood me, and there was no way he was going to 'sprag' on me to the authorities. So much for the patient, caring and peace-loving teacher and mother. I turned and left the room, told the office I had a severe migraine and went home.

When Chris arrived back, about five-thirty, I was sitting in the front room in the half-light, the curtains not drawn and the fire not yet lit.

'What's up Mum? Are you alright?' He flung his bag and his jacket onto the table, looking worried and a little embarrassed; anything 'female' made him ill at ease, although he had been very supportive all the time I had been unwell the previous year.

'Chris, do you think I'm a good mother?' How needy and pathetic I sounded.

He was immediately and understandably irritated. 'What sort of a question is that? How do I know what a good mother is? I dunno... yeh, I suppose you are... of course you are...' He softened. 'Sorry about this morning. I know I get you riled and you're not meant to get upset. What's the matter? Are you poorly?'

'Oh, it's nothing really. I came back from school early. Migraine.'

'Right, I'll get you one of your tablets shall I?' Chris sounded relieved; he liked things to be clear, hated ambiguity.

'Yes, thanks. They're on the kitchen table. And get me a glass of water.'

The room was nearly dark now. It was soothing; I closed my eyes and let the evening sounds wash over me. Papers thudding through letter boxes, the click-clack of heels on the pavement, strains of the news at 5:45. My thoughts were half-formed and hazy and I drifted...

Just after I'd started work, I'd set Jacko's class a piece of writing on their Christmas holidays. The banality of the task was matched by most of the efforts, which had merely consisted of lists of expensive gifts: laptops, Xboxes, iPods and the like. Jacko had gripped a stub of pencil in his fist and had laboriously produced a few closely-written lines dug into the paper. I'd later managed, with his help, to decipher the fact that he'd received a tin of Cadbury's *Heroes* from his Mum.

'It wasn't one of them small 'uns though Miss. It was huge and I gave little 'uns two goodies each. There was a game inside as well but I couldn't work it out. Me Mam threw the tin out by mistake and I was going to keep my stuff in it.'

Poor kid. Deprived kid. Did his mother love him? Did she think she was a good mother? Did he? Perhaps she was just very tired...

Chris came back into the room carrying the glass and my tablets. As he opened the door, the light from the hall clearly illuminated his features. I felt as though I was in the darkened wings and he was the principal actor, centre stage. He certainly had the looks to be an actor – he was small but sturdy and clean-cut with that steady gaze. My eyelids were heavy but as I looked up at him I caught sight of what I thought was...

'What's that mark on the side of your face, Chris? Have you been fighting or has someone hit you?'

But I was sleepy, and maybe my question was spoken too softly for him to hear. At any rate, he didn't answer but set the glass and tablets down on a small table beside me. And just before I closed my eyes again, I saw that intense gaze of Jacko and Chris fixed on me like two photographic prints that had superimposed.

# T-Junction

The bus slowly nosed its way up the High Street. Elizabeth rubbed at the grimy window to clear a space through which to peer. She had been obliged to sit near the back of the bus – there had been few free places and her legs ached from an afternoon of intensive shopping – and the air hung heavy with smoke. Crumbly ash flecked the red vinyl seat, and she carefully placed her well-polished court shoes on the bar below the one directly in front so as to avoid tab ends that littered the floor like shrivelled grubs. She felt suspended in this static murkiness amid the grey sculpted figures of her fellow passengers, who hunched into their newspapers or stared wordlessly ahead.

The bus came to a halt and she saw that it had reached the T-junction at the end of the small market town, after which it turned left, if it was a 47, to head towards the coast and right, if a 47A, to go inland, winding its way through the many hamlets and villages of the Yorkshire Dales. The one-way street was narrow at this point and she found herself looking directly into the front window of a small antiques shop, which must have opened recently as she had no recollection of having noticed it before. Idly, by force of habit almost as much as anything else, she gazed over the display. In fact, display was hardly the appropriate term for the items cluttered there: clocks, oddments of crockery (some chipped and stained), a smeared glass case containing pieces of costume jewellery on a crumpled bit of black velvet, some genuine Victorian bric-a-brac side by side with cheap imported basketware, piles of what looked like old theatre programmes, cigarette cards and motorcycle magazines, a cricket bat, and miniature bottles in sludgy green, blue and brown. In the middle loomed a large, rather attractive painted firescreen with one of its feet missing so that it lurched to one side, a lacy shawl slung over the top; and propped against that, a plastic framed picture of a Spanish flamenco dancer in garish unreal colours, the mouth a crimson slash in her flat clay-like face, brown arms held angularly like those of a puppet. The window bowed out like a protuberant eye, and above it the beetling frontage made it look as if the whole shop were scowling at her. 'Old Father Tyme' proclaimed the lettering on the door, accompanied by a silhouette of a disagreeable old man brandishing a scythe and an hourglass.

Then, just as a grinding of gears and hissing exhalation of air indicated the bus's intention to move off, she caught a fleeting impression of something slightly apart from the rest of the goods, presumably metallic from the way it had appeared to wink at her from the corner of the window as the bus turned right and the shop slipped back out of sight. For some reason it aroused her interest, and she decided to call in the next time she was passing. Rearranging her assortment of glossy carrier bags, she settled back for the rest of the short journey.

Her next visit to town, for her regular wash and blow dry, was a week later, and after a quick coffee and cream éclair in 'Ye Olde Coffee Shoppe' she made her way to Old Father Tyme. The contents of the window seemed unchanged and the object of her mission was still wedged right against the glass in the corner. She would have supposed the shop to have been closed had it not been for the scruffy 'Open' sign swinging on the door. Cautiously she pushed against it and entered the small dark interior. The owner, sitting behind a dusty counter and puffing fetid clouds of smoke into the gloom, looked as though he might have been the model for the figure on the door – wizened, stooped, the corners of his eyes and mouth pulled downwards.

'Yes?' His voice was surprisingly high-pitched.

'I'd like to look at something in the window, please.'

He raised a bushy eyebrow in query.

'A sort of metal thing, like a plaque...' She shaped it in the air with her hands, feeling awkward and annoyed at his silence and lack of bonhomie.

With a deep sigh he hoisted himself off the stool and shuffled over to the window. She pointed and he reached forward, knocking a jug over as he did and not bothering to replace it. He pushed the object at her rudely. It was an old gilt frame, about eight inches square, with a heart-shaped space in the middle for a picture or photograph. Ornate scrolls, flowers and cupids embossed the surround making it look vulgar and sentimental. Yet it still appealed, and she was able to envisage a photograph of the family in the frame as a present for Robert on Valentine's Day, also their anniversary. She would be dismissive about it, laugh carelessly to show it was just a whimsical act of self-indulgence but in truth it would serve as a symbolic celebration of their marriage and children, Charles and Sophie, aged twelve and ten respectively.

'How much is it?' she asked, turning the frame over and noticing that the backing was loose and would need fixing.

His hooded eyes met hers briefly, then slid away. '£50.'

'Goodness!' Startled, she traced its embossed decorations with one leather-gloved finger. She was not an expert, but she guessed that price was far in excess of its value. Reluctantly she handed it back to him.

He shrugged and shoved the frame back in the window.

Elizabeth was unsettled as she went about the rest of her shopping, paying regulation calls at butcher, chemist, ironmonger and deli. She was so distracted she almost boarded the wrong bus, something she had always dreaded. One of her recurrent nightmares, along with going out in her bedroom slippers or making a fool of herself by misunderstanding something foreign on a menu, was of mistakenly catching a 47 bus and being unable to alight until its destination.

Why, she asked herself as she unlocked the front door of their home – a four-bedroomed detached pseudo-Georgian residence on an exclusive estate just outside the town – why such a feeling of disappointment and frustration? There was no reason she should not buy the frame, despite its price. Robert was now a partner in the town's small but successful firm of estate agents, which ensured they had no financial worries. What was the limit to which she would have gone – £10, £20, £30?

A little later, drinking a cup of tea in the new kitchen (dark oak units with granite worktops), Elizabeth found herself unable to dislodge the inclination to buy the frame. She could just imagine it, polished and glowing, standing on Robert's dark oak desk in his study, bathed in the muted light of the table lamp next to it. The four of them encased in gold, smiling out from the plump heart-shaped frame, solid, immovable. It was too tempting. She decided to return the next day and get it.

Unfortunately this proved impossible, as in the morning it became obvious that both children were running a temperature and, indeed, this proved to signal the onset of a severe bout of 'flu. Once they were well, she had to go and look after her mother in Mablethorpe who had fallen on her way home from Bingo and hurt her back. By the time she had returned, and coped with the backlog of laundry and other domestic chores, it was the beginning of February. At the first opportunity, she hurried back to the shop and found Old Father Tyme as loquacious as ever,

'Sold!' he squeaked tersely.

By February 14th Old Father Tyme, both shop and owner, had gone. Newspapers had been stuck to the inside of the whitened glass, 'For Sale' posters to the outside. Over their special meal that evening of Thai green curry followed by profiteroles, Elizabeth asked Robert about the shop's sudden demise. He claimed no knowledge of the property and said, laughingly, that anyway she knew it was his rule never to mix business and pleasure. It was their custom to save the exchange of gifts until after coffee when the children were safely in bed. Now, as she sank back into an armchair and flicked through a magazine, Elizabeth felt mellow from the half bottle of Beaujolais that warmed her veins.

Yawning and laying aside the magazine, she watched her husband standing at the other side of the room, at the corner cocktail bar running his finger along the row of squat jewel-coloured liqueur bottles. They had recently affixed two squares of mirror tiles on each of the walls that made the right-angle of the corner and to Elizabeth, half-closing her eyes, they looked like the two silver pages of an open book. By moving her head first one way then the other she could see Robert's profile doubly reflected. As he poured out cherry brandy, the viscous ruby liquid trickling thickly into crystal glasses, she inclined her head to the left and dreamily considered the image in the right-hand mirror.

As she did so Robert held one of the glasses up against the light as if he were a priest blessing the Communion wine.

She thought of that magazine story she'd read in which, at a moment of irresolution, the hero had turned to the woman, swept her into his arms and, bruising her lips with his, had transported them both into timeless realms of ecstasy. Letting her thoughts run freely and hazily through this pink-fringed world, she could just imagine Robert bringing out a small square package that would contain the photograph frame, the perfect counterpoint to her abortive romantic gesture. She knew the look they would exchange and, later, how that look would be translated into a night of tender love-making, a rich resonance of all the passion throughout the twelve years of their marriage.

Robert replaced the glass on top of the cabinet and bent down to open the doors of the cupboard underneath, where he always stored her present. He delved into it, pretending to have lost the gift. She laughed dutifully.

Turning her head the other way, the image in the left hand mirror was not as distinct and momentarily could have been that of a stranger. It kindled a mental picture that panicked her: where it came from she had no idea. Robert was lying naked on top of his secretary, pinning her to the floor of an empty building like a butterfly to a board. Her hands fluttered down and over his back then clutched wildly as their two bodies arched together. Heart thudding, Elizabeth could almost taste the smells of sweat, paint and sawdust chasing round the stuffy, shuttered room. She saw the photograph frame, standing on a bedside table of baby-pink ruffles, defiled by the picture it held. Gleaming flesh. Scraps of black lace. Loose tumble of hair. Provocative partly-open mouth. She shrank back in the chair and brushed her hand across her eyes, wanting to wipe away the dirt that clouded her vision. Struggling, all she could manage to see now was the familiar picture of Robert bringing out a small square package containing a bottle of her favourite perfume that he gave her every year, the exact counterpart to the bottle of aftershave she had bought for him. She knew how their eyes would avoid one another and how, later, their quick dry coupling would be a hollow echo of the years that yawned behind them.

Robert straightened up and turned towards her, holding a square package gift-wrapped in silver and gold spangled paper. He smiled.

Then, as if there were mirrors within mirrors multiplying smaller and smaller images into the distance, she saw in the right hand ones Sophie and Charles, miniature replicas of her and Robert. Charles was standing behind a seated Sophie, his arm resting protectively on her shoulder and smiling straight ahead. Sophie, hands laced demurely in her lap, had her face half-turned upwards to look at him. Assurance and success framed them.

Robert walked across the living room towards her, the sound of his footsteps muffled by the deep pile carpet.

Jerking her head the other way she saw, in the left hand mirrors, both children positioned as before but with their features gently distorted. Charles still smiled but his lips seemed thinner, his eyes steelier. Sophie looked almost frightened, as if his grip on her shoulder was hurting. The frame this time was that of a cage.

Her head swam as she looked up at Robert, now standing directly above her, proffering the glittering parcel.

'Happy anniversary, darling.'

That night she dreamt of deliberately taking the 47 bus to the coast, of standing on the cliffs of broken jagged teeth and watching the angry North Sea punch and batter its way into the heart of the countryside.

# Lost

I'd lost my mother and was therefore in somewhat of a tizz. She'd been very vague recently and prone to drifting off into a world of her own, so it was no great surprise, but nevertheless it was only natural that one should feel a bit anxious. As soon as I realised she wasn't there (and for goodness sake, I'd only popped out to spend a penny and put some powder on) I felt that awful flush spread from my chest and seep up onto my neck and face. True it was a terribly hot day, indeed the weatherman that morning had said the hottest in August since records began, but my heat came from within. I knew that I must look like an absolute beetroot (so much for the powder), but that didn't stop me rushing out to the front desk and asking the rather gormless girl on duty there if she'd seen Mummy. The girl looked at me as if I was some kind of mental defective, and I resolved to speak to Matron about her the following morning. What they teach them in schools nowadays heaven alone knows, but it certainly isn't communication skills, that's for sure. No doubt they sit O-levels, or rather G.C.S.E.'s, in drug taking and sexual intercourse.

I presumed she'd be wandering round the garden. They did keep the garden nice at the Home, I have to say. It had been professionally landscaped with a good display of shrubs but lots of colourful bedding plants too. Old people always like that. They'd laid paths, nice and smooth for the wheelchairs, and benches every so often so that inmates could just sit and contemplate. Mummy loved her garden; when she was at home, I mean. She used to spend hours just pottering about, trowel in hand, with one of her many ridiculous hats on. She'd certainly got green fingers, no doubt about that! Everything she planted just ran amok: in the summer, troughs, pots and hanging baskets spilled over with blooms. It was the same with her paintings; I was forever finding canvases stashed away in the garden shed, or behind a chest of drawers. Of course in recent years, her eyesight was poor so she needed to virtually stick her head in a flower before she knew what it was, and rest her nose against a painting to see what she'd done. I used to find that terribly annoying for some reason. Not fair, I know, because she couldn't help that anymore than she could help wetting the bed or dribbling her food. It was just the body shutting down.

As soon as I was outside, a wall of heat hit me and I had to shade my eyes. I thought I spotted her just by the buddleia in the corner of the walled garden. She loved the butterflies, you see, and if you let her would spend hours watching them flit to and fro. Mummy was always an observer; she could just sit and look at a view, or a work of art or whatever, and to be quite honest it used to make me a bit twitchy. I suppose it's because I'm more what you might call a doer. Always have been ever since my schooldays – member of the hockey, netball and rounders team, the Church choir, a patrol leader in Guides. Did my Duke of Edinburgh Gold and was secretary of Junior Branch of the Round Table. It's the same now. I can't bear just to be sitting. Even if I'm in front of the television – not that there's anything worth watching these days – I'll make sure I've got some ironing to do.

Anyway, as I said, I was sure it was Mummy until I got a bit closer and realised it was Frieda from the room two doors down the corridor. They're about the same height and stature so it was an understandable error on my part.

'Hello there Frieda!' I called out cheerily, and gave her a big wave as she slowly shifted herself round on her walking frame to face me. It's terribly important, I feel, to be cheerful when you're with old people. 'It's me, Sheila! I'm looking for my mother. Have you seen her?' Perhaps she hadn't heard, as she gave no reply, so I tried again.

'Frieda! Have you seen Alice? You know Alice. My mother? I've lost her.'

She shook her head before laboriously turning herself around again. She was obviously going a bit doolally like so many of them in the place. Tragic really.

Next I decided to try the paper shop a few hundred yards down from the main gate. I turned up the collar of my shirt in an attempt to shield my neck from the sun as I strode out. Mummy went there every day, sometimes more than once, to fetch her copy of *The Independent* and buy a bag of Mint Imperials or anything else that caught her eye. She didn't need to; the Home had offered to have the paper and anything else she wanted delivered, but typically she refused. I'm of the opinion that it was a way of making a public declaration of independence. I'd say to her:

'Mummy, we should swap places. I'd give my eye teeth to have my shopping delivered instead of having to traipse round after work, or dash out from the office in my lunch hour.'

Then she'd reply, in that rather tart way she had, that she'd be delighted to swap but that she was hardly in a position to do any negotiating about where she should live and what she should do with the remainder of her life. Mummy's mental faculties, I have to say, remained undimmed by old age. Her riposte was a reference to the fact that she not gone into the Home voluntarily. Matron explained to me that this was very common – people who for most of their lives had been very caring, sensitive souls couldn't seem to appreciate, when old, just what effect looking after them was having on their carers. I liked that word 'carer'. I was my mother's carer and as such I had rights as well as responsibilities. Mummy hadn't liked me attending the Carers Support Group every Wednesday evening at the Community Centre. Well of course she hadn't! It was there that I met the likes of Gail and Mandy, who had encouraged me to stand up for myself a bit more.

'You're never going to get yourself a man in your present situation, Sheila,' Gail had told me earnestly during the coffee break on my third visit to the group.

'And what about babies?' Mandy asked.

Frankly, at the age of forty-six, not only did I feel myself to be a bit past it for sprogging but I wasn't even sure whether I liked kiddywinks. However, I didn't say anything to my new friends. They were only trying to help, and anyway there was a principle at stake.

'It's a very common situation,' Gail had explained. 'Society assumes the spinster daughter will care for the surviving parent or parents, thus sacrificing her own future. When that parent dies, it's too late for the carer to forge a life of her own.'

I loved that word 'forge'. It sounded so heroic! I saw myself forging for all I was worth. Repeating that word to myself allowed me to get through the awful business of finding a Home and getting Mummy moved out. Gail and Mandy had promised to help, but when it came to the crunch they found that they were too busy with their own families. The trouble was I'd envisaged so many changes happening afterwards; I had plans for redecorating and refurbishing the house, and had pictured myself having friends round for lunch or dinner. I thought I'd be free to go out a lot more myself, perhaps join a few groups or societies, and then possibly meet someone who would become special to me.

But it didn't happen and I can't really explain why. The thing was, my days still seemed to revolve around Mummy even when she wasn't there. Naturally I'd go to visit every day after work, and by the time I got home I was too tired to do much. At weekends I'd spend either the morning or the afternoon at the

Home, and the rest of my time seemed to entail getting caught up with housework. We'd had a Home Help when Mummy was there so I hadn't had to do much of that sort of thing before. The garden, Mummy's pride and joy, quickly became overrun with weeds and I didn't seem to be able to keep on top of that either. Actually, if the truth be known, my mother had been right when she'd said I was pretty useless. She urged me not to come so often to visit, but I wasn't going to give her the opportunity to accuse me of neglect.

Speaking of neglect, that's precisely what the Home had been guilty of I thought as, puffing and panting, I raked my gaze up and down the road outside the paper shop. Having drawn a blank, I decided to take the shortcut across the field to the Rose and Crown where Mummy had been known to pop in from time to time for a gin and tonic. The grass was brown and dry and scratched my bare legs and unfortunately, I snagged my cardigan on some brambles, not to mention standing in a couple of crusted cow pats, but nevertheless the time saved was worth it. However, it was the same story at the pub. When I asked if anyone had seen Mummy, the rather nice woman behind the bar asked me if I'd like to sit down and have a cold drink. Perhaps I was a trifle ungracious, but I replied rather brusquely that when you have lost your mother you cannot spare the time to sit around in a public house having a drink, as if it were a social occasion.

My next port of call was the little pottery where she loved to browse but, being in a flap, I managed to knock a couple of pieces off the display stand, one of which, I regret to say, shattered, showering my shoes and skirt with a fine coating of plaster dust. I was dimly aware of a man's raised voice but I took no notice as by now I was beginning to get seriously worried.

Hurriedly retracing my route back to the Home, feeling the sweat trickling down my armpits and rubbing at the waistband of my skirt, I found Matron standing on the step waiting for me. I was dimly aware of a couple of other people standing behind her. Goodness knows what I looked like – a terrible sight, no doubt, what with my scratched legs, dirty shoes, the plaster dust and my red face. She came towards me with her arms outstretched (she was a kindly woman) and said: 'Sheila, come in and sit down. You're very upset and it's so hot. I'm going to make you a nice glass of iced tea.'

Her hands were lovely and cool. She put one onto my forehead and wiped a strand of my damp hair aside. I used to do that with Mummy, though her hair was always dry and rather wispy. (Only when she was asleep, though, she didn't like me touching her when she was awake.)

'Have you found her?' I asked.

'No, Sheila, we haven't. Come inside now, it's not good for you being out in this heat."

'I just can't think where she might be,' I said.

'She's gone, Sheila, you know that. Come on in now.'

'Gone?'

There was a pause. A vein throbbed in my forehead.

'You lost your mother a fortnight ago now. Alice died. You remember that don't you?'

I remembered, of course. I remembered the smell of the hearse and the burnished wood of the coffin and the hymns that we sang and the flowers that were leaned up drunkenly against the wall of the crematorium.

'You've had a bit of a funny turn, not surprising in this weather. It's very natural to be disorientated when you've lost someone close to you.'

I got lost at the seaside once when I was just a tiny tot. It had been a scorcher of a day, just like this one. Mummy had been absorbed in her book and I'd wandered off with my bucket looking for shells. There was always a pretty one just a bit further on, and before I knew it I had strayed far from our picnic rug. After what seemed like hours, but was in all probability only about twenty minutes or so, I straightened up. Looking round all I could see was a vast expanse of sand, patchworked with families who were frighteningly unfamiliar. I'd lost Mummy. A feeling of blind panic swamped me and I had to crouch down to stop my legs shaking whereupon, to my utter shame, I couldn't prevent stop myself wetting my pants. Then I howled. Naturally it wasn't long before I was scooped up, fussed over and taken to the Lifeguard's 'Lost and Found' tent. Mummy was very cross with me, in itself a rare occurrence, and I gloried in the attention despite the upset.

'You weren't lost!' she said. 'You knew where you were didn't you?'

'On the beach,' I'd sobbed.

'And I was on the beach too. It was just that we were further apart than you'd thought. All that fuss! If you're that worried about being separated from me you'd better stay close.'

And that's what I did, Mummy. For forty-six years I stayed as close as I could, even when I could sense you didn't really want me there.

'Sheila?' A hand on my arm, gentle pressure persuading me to shade and coolness inside. But I shook it off, turning round and thrusting my face upwards to the sun so that I could feel my skin burn just as hers must have done. A very slight breeze ruffled the air, and my nostrils caught on it the faintest trace of autumnal decay, rotting leaves, woodsmoke; a crackling as bones and wood snapped and a cave of red embers streamed blood down its sides. From somewhere else I heard a great cry of pain, like an animal gives when released from a trap. The cry rises in pitch and volume as the animal struggles to drag its damaged body forward. Under the beating sun its limbs are floppy, its mouth parched. There is a sensation of rushing water, a falling and then blackness.

# Dabblers

Ann, Claire and Sheila. All dabblers. Dabble, dabble, muddle, paddle as they splash around in the shallows, occasionally standing ankle-deep in the swirling water, very rarely venturing knee-deep, certainly never fully immersing themselves.

*WARNING – STRONG CURRENTS*
*WARNING – DANGEROUS WATERS*
*WARNING – POWERFUL UNDERTOW*

Ann was a nurse. Still is, come to that, but she doesn't work anymore. It would be difficult to fit in round the children, so she says. Perhaps when they're older. She did once get a part-time job at the local Health Centre, but Louise and Emily complained about her not being there when they got home from school. Before she left in the early afternoon, she'd put a salad out for Andrew to have after he came back tired from evening surgery. He was never openly critical – but the limp lettuce and rubbery quiche, left largely untouched on the plate, were reproach enough. After four months she left.

She started the Open University Foundation Course and found it easily within her capabilities, but it was difficult finding time to do the assignments. When the dates of the summer school were announced and she found they clashed with those of their annual camping holiday in Brittany, she felt justified in abandoning her studies. After all, she could always pick them up again in the future.

She was a parent governor at the girls' school and helped with the summer and Christmas fayres, organised a jumble sale to raise funds for a mini-bus and dutifully attended concerts, sports days and open days. She took her turn to host handicraft sessions held monthly in one of the committee members' houses, amid the clatter of coffee cups and the deft click, tick, snip of needles and scissors. The talk, on the respective merits of each other's solar panels, organic veg boxes and children (usually in that order) lapped reassuringly at Ann's feet. Once a week she attended the local FE college where she did an evening class in Word Processing. Her tutor had said she was coming along very nicely and wanted her to take some exams, but Ann was doubtful. If Andrew was called out on an emergency she would have to miss the class. Anyway, she'd never been any good at exams, she explained to her tutor as she agitated her mug of grey tepid coffee. Splosh, splish, splosh.

She and Claire, her neighbour, had talked about setting up a nursery. Ann had loved the thought of being able to cuddle all those babies. They had even got as far as investigating possible premises and exploring ways of financing it. Business Enterprise Schemes. Grants. Ann had bought a bright orange folder especially for the paperwork. Now it lay forgotten under a stack of unread books on the windowsill of Andrew's study, its bright orange cover bleached by the sunlight to a dull mustard. Not that both of them had ever taken a decision to abandon the project; it had simply faded, like the cover of the folder, until it merely hovered like summer's mist on the periphery of both women's mental landscape. It was soon displaced by an idea to open an organic cafe, then to run a soft toy business from home, then to try for the franchise for a nappy delivering service. Andrew listened patiently to Ann outlining all these schemes, and was careful to offer no objection but no encouragement either.

Yet part of her, the greater part, was content. She had all she had ever wished for. It was only rarely, as she pottered round her comfortable family home, that she would experience a longing, a yearning for something else impossible to localise. She couldn't point to where it hurt, like Andrew's patients did, so she administered to herself more of the same medicine. She had decided, she told Andrew one night in bed, to take Yoga next term and possibly an A-level in Psychology at the college.

'Mmmm... why not?' Andrew said, leaning on one elbow above her and running his hands over her body, his mouth stopping further talk. She'd always liked his bedside manner. Possibilities rippled pleasurably over and into her, one after the other, like his fingers.

Claire thought a job would be the answer for Ann, choosing to ignore the fact that her own gave little satisfaction. A maths teacher at the same school where Alec, her husband, was the deputy head, she felt restless. The years rolled by in a repeating pattern – three terms, sliced through the middle by half-term, two weeks at Easter and Christmas, six in the summer. Always she seemed to be anticipating the next block of school or holiday, always living outside time, feeling as if she was standing on the bank watching it flow past like a huge, powerful river. Desperately, she tried to dissipate her feelings of frustration into physical activity. She played netball, squash, did circuit training three times a week and swam every morning. Slash, splash, splash. Still she felt charged with unused energy.

She and Alec had moved round the country as Alec pursued his headship. She had always had to fit in round him, job-wise, after he had secured his next promotion. Consequently, she had a lot of teaching experience but little to show in terms of career status. Temporary contracts. Covers for maternity leave. A term at home to redecorate the hall. Periodic supply work. Alec had made his moves shrewdly and they had benefited from the boom in property values. Ann was openly envious of Claire's detached house, the biggest in the close: five bedrooms, two with en-suite bathrooms, it was set slightly back from the others and fronted by mature trees, while a balcony on the master bedroom looked over open fields at the back. Inside, polish and fresh flowers lightly scented the air; feet left gentle indentations on the deep pile carpets, which then discreetly eased themselves back into shape. Curtains in classic prints, co-ordinating with suites, papers and borders, swished back to reveal spotless picture windows. The fitted kitchen was in dark oak, the dining room in pine, the bathrooms tiled in aquamarine. And Claire did take pleasure in it, the planning, the choosing, the translation of her concepts into this statement of good taste. She would sometimes glide from room to room, touching her furniture and fabrics, and feel pride in the fact it was all hers.

She tried attributing her feeling of restlessness to the absence of children, and for a while she had come off the Pill to see if anything happened. But it didn't, and it was with relief that she returned to the clinic to pick up a further six months supply. She and Alec told themselves it was obviously not meant to be, and Claire's nightmares of her lovely home in total disorder, smelling of shit and pee and all the doors locked with her and the baby trapped inside, ceased as suddenly as they had appeared. She resolved to try and appreciate her good fortune and started working for Oxfam on a Saturday morning, sorting bundles of smelly clothes and making bright conversation with the genteel elderly ladies who made up the rest of the staff and who were touchingly curious about her husband and their social life. Occasionally she would run home Elsie and Madge who shared the sorting with her. Both were widows. Elsie lived in a shabby Edwardian terrace down an avenue which was now largely student houses. She complained with good humour of their noise, but was reluctant to move. She liked to have the space for when her sons and their families visited, although this was not as often as she would like. They were all very busy people. Mind you, she was busy too, she assured Claire, what with all her Church activities and voluntary work. Madge, on the other hand, lived in a new sheltered housing development, though she had little time for her fellow residents.

'Terribly boring, my dear,' she confided to Claire one Saturday after they had dropped Elsie off and both, by tacit agreement, then felt free to light up. She missed her husband. Her life had centred on looking after him and their home, the focal point of her day being the preparation and serving of his evening meal. He had dropped dead at the age of fifty-eight just before he was due to retire from his own business. There had never been any children and somehow she'd never had many other interests of her own. Well, one didn't then, not like the young modern women of today. But there seemed such a void, such a gaping void. Now she felt she was simply filling in time.

Claire felt the resonance of Madge's words vibrate in her bones and shivered.

Ann had met Sheila at a school function and had subsequently introduced her to Claire. Sheila's house was only a few minutes' walk from the other two women's, but in sharp contrast. A crumbling end-of-row terrace, it was easy to imagine the slight curve of its outside wall to be a bulge arising from its many occupants. Sheila and her husband Daz had four children with another one imminent. It was difficult to know with Sheila when one pregnancy ended and another started. She wore voluminous flowing clothes and one or more children were always attached at hip or breast. She appeared fluid, her long auburn hair whipping around her face, her skirt of Indian cotton streaming behind her as she strode along with laden pram. Daz was an artist and it was this bohemian element, as well as the fact that Sheila herself had done two years at art school (stopping because of the arrival of Toby, her eldest) that, in the eyes of Ann and Claire, set her apart from the swarm of mothers who buzzed daily between shops, school and home.

Sheila was apparently the archetypal Earth Mother; she loved her children passionately, loved conceiving them, carrying them, delivering them and caring for them. Her house was a welter of toys, clean and dirty clothes, bibs, bits of half-eaten food, bottles, prams, high-chairs, baby walkers, push-a-longs and building bricks. Paintings were blu-tacked to undecorated walls, ill-shod feet clattered on uncarpeted stairs and the steamy kitchen fermented with wine, bread and chatter. She drifted through it all, a dreamy look on her face, making endless cups of coffee, lighting a cigarette then letting it burn forgotten in an ashtray while she sorted out some domestic fracas. She soothed and comforted, rarely lost her temper and almost let the tide of motherhood wash over her head. And yet. Sometimes while giving the night feed, deep, deep down in the dark stillness of her soul an undercurrent of longing would tug at her with the same insistence as the baby's mouth on her nipple. She would unplug the infant and lay it back in its crib, letting the milk leak down her body unchecked. Dribble. Trickle. Dribble. Then she'd creep up to the loft which had been converted into a studio for Daz. The only painting she'd done since having the children was to decorate the studio in the shades of green which Daz found conducive for working, but some of her old canvases were still stacked in a corner. She would squat on the floor and, one by one, would wipe the dust off and kiss them as if they were photographs of old lovers. Then, animal-like, she'd crawl round and sniff at the paints and brushes and bottles of turps. Raw need would jab her in the groin like lust and so she'd return to bed with Daz, snug up tightly behind his curved back and move against him, translating her fleshless desire into one they both understood. In due course her belly would once again swell, and the arrival of another baby would postpone the need to make a decision about what to do when the children were older.

Daz's income was erratic and she'd done a variety of badly-paid part-time jobs: office cleaner, care assistant, lollipop lady, shop work. They offered her little, but she expected nothing so could accept the disdain of her employers with equanimity. Only occasionally did her A-levels in Art, English and History, distant markers of her past, loom through the fog of time to mock her. She ran the community playgroup with ease, and it was to her that Claire and Ann had originally come with their idea for the nursery. They'd talked about it a lot, all three of them, over coffee and wine and they seemed to have all the necessary starting ingredients. Ann and Claire both had some capital, Ann had the requisite nursing qualifications, Claire the educational input and Sheila the practical experience of running something similar. There was nothing really holding them back. But it never happened. Why not?

Well, the warning signs were there. They'd watched the men wade into the wide, angry sea, plough through the waves, swallow water, choke, but hold their heads up and fight on. Truly it was not that of which they were afraid. After all, those men were only Andrew, Alec and Daz in different guises. And Andrew, Alec and Daz, despite their faults, had never hit their wives, had never been unfaithful (well, hardly ever) and worked to the best of their abilities to be good, loyal, loving husbands. The water might well be deep and cold and rough – or so the men would like to have them believe – but it could be difficult standing on the edge as well.

No, being a dabbler is for Ann, Claire and Sheila (and Madge and Elsie) the crux of their unwillingness to be initiators. It stops them taking the big plunge, makes them continually wait and watch on the shore rather than participate. Arguably, it is a supportive role they have been conditioned into, that of eternal backstage helper and understudy to their menfolk. But it is their strength too; the source of a vital strength that enables them to explore, to challenge, to question and eventually to discover. It is at this point of discovery that the many and diverse threads of their lives are able to entwine into a thick cable of purpose that will prove to be their lifeline.

Thus:

Many years later, Sheila left her family in order to complete her studies and become a painter. She moved to London and was quite successful, in fact much more so than Daz had ever been. Claire became a freelance interior designer and worked on different projects around the country. Alec's time was divided between his duties as headmaster and waiting for Claire to phone him. Sometimes she rang him from Sheila's London house, where she often stayed. The two women had forged links neither would have dreamt of in their younger days. As for Ann, she never resumed a career but had two more children, she and Andrew then adopting a further two.

And maybe this is no more than further dabbling. Maybe at the end of the day Ann, Claire and Sheila still hear the distant boom of the sea in their ears, as a reminder of what might have been. Who knows? Not even I, a dabbler in writing, and someone who has been each one of these women at some point or other in my life. But do the men really do any better? To extend the metaphor well beyond the bounds of stylistic decency – they either drown (Madge and Elsie's husbands), tread water (Alec), are abandoned in mid-ocean (Daz) or are waterlogged by the demands of their dependants (Andrew). Maybe those warning signs were of our own making. Maybe all us dabblers should hold hands, make a chain out into the water and pull everyone in?

Maybe.